A Christmas Carol

Charles Dickens

A WATERMILL CLASSIC

Contents

Stave One
Marley's Ghost

Marley was dead, to begin with. There is no doubt whatever about that. The register of his burial was signed by the clergyman, the clerk, the undertaker, and the chief mourner. Scrooge signed it. And Scrooge's name was good upon 'Change for anything he chose to put his hand to.

Old Marley was as dead as a doornail.

Mind! I don't mean to say that I know, of my own knowledge, what there is particularly dead about a doornail. I might have been inclined, myself, to regard a coffin-nail as the deadest piece of ironmongery in the trade. But the wisdom of our ancestors is in the simile; and my unhallowed hands shall not disturb it, or the Country's done for. You will therefore permit me to repeat, emphatically, that Marley was as dead as a doornail.

Scrooge knew he was dead? Of course he did. How could it be otherwise? Scrooge and he were partners for I don't know how many years. Scrooge was his sole executor, his sole administrator, his sole assign, his sole residuary legatee, his sole friend, and sole mourner. And even Scrooge was not so dreadfully cut up by the sad event, but that he was an excellent man of business on the very day of the funeral, and solemnized it with an undoubted bargain.

The mention of Marley's funeral brings me back to the point I started from. There is no doubt that Marley was dead. This must be distinctly understood, or nothing wonderful can come of the story I am going to relate. If we were not convinced that Hamlet's father died before the play began, there would be nothing more remarkable in his taking a stroll at night, in an easterly wind, upon his own ramparts, than there would be in any other middle-aged gentleman rashly turning out after dark in a breezy spot—say Saint Paul's Churchyard for instance—literally to astonish his son's weak mind.

Scrooge never painted out old Marley's name. There it stood, years afterward, above the warehouse door: Scrooge and Marley. The firm was known as Scrooge and Marley. Sometimes people new to the business called Scrooge Scrooge, and sometimes Marley, but he answered to both names. It was all the same to him.

Oh! but he was a tight-fisted hand at the grindstone, Scrooge! a squeezing, wrenching, grasping, scraping, clutching, covetous old sinner! Hard and sharp as flint, from which no steel had ever struck out generous fire, secret, and self-contained, and solitary as an oyster. The cold within him froze his old features, nipped his pointed nose, shriveled his cheek, stiffened his gait, made his eyes red, his thin lips blue, and spoke out shrewdly in his grating voice. A frosty rime was on his head, and on his eyebrows, and his wiry chin. He carried his own low temperature always about with him; he iced his office in the dog-days; and didn't thaw it one degree at Christmas.

External heat and cold had little influence on Scrooge. No warmth could warm, no wintry weather chill him. No wind that blew was bitterer than he, no falling snow was more intent upon its purpose, no pelting rain less open to entreaty. Foul weather didn't know where to have him. The heaviest rain, and snow, and hail, and sleet, could boast of the advantage over him in only one respect. They often "came down" handsomely, and Scrooge never did.

Nobody ever stopped him in the street to say, with gladsome looks, "My dear Scrooge, how are you? When will you come to see me?" No beggars implored him how to bestow a trifle, no children asked him what it was o'clock, no man or woman ever once in all his life inquired the way to such and such a place, of Scrooge. Even the blind men's dogs appeared to know him; and, when they saw him coming on, would tug their owners into doorways and up courts; and then would wag their tails as though they said, "No eye at all is better than an evil eye, dark master!"

But what did Scrooge care? It was the very thing he liked. To edge his way along the crowded paths of life, warning all human sympathy to keep its distance, was what the knowing ones call "nuts" to Scrooge.

Once upon a time—of all the good days in the year, on Christmas Eve—old Scrooge sat busy in his counting-house. It was cold, bleak, biting weather, foggy withal, and he could hear the people in the court outside go wheezing up and down, beating their hands upon their breasts, and stamping their feet upon the pavement stones to warm them. The city clocks had only just gone three, but it was quite dark already—it had not been light all day—and candles were flaring in the windows of the neighboring offices, like ruddy smears upon the palpable brown air. The fog came pouring in at every chink and keyhole, and was so dense without, that, although the court was of the narrowest, the houses opposite were mere phantoms. To see the dingy cloud come drooping down, obscuring everything, one might have thought that Nature lived hard by, and was brewing on a large scale.

The door of Scrooge's counting-house was open, that he might keep his eye upon his clerk, who, in a dismal little cell beyond, a sort of tank, was copying letters. Scrooge had a very small fire, but the clerk's fire was so very much smaller that it looked like one coal. But he couldn't replenish it, for Scrooge kept the coal-box in his own room, and so surely as the clerk came in with the shovel, the master predicted that it would be necessary for them to part. Wherefore the clerk put on his white comforter, and tried to warm himself at the candle; in which effort, not being a man of a strong imagination, he failed.

"A Merry Christmas, uncle! God save you!" cried a cheerful voice. It was the voice of Scrooge's nephew, who came upon him so quickly that this was the first intimation he had of his approach.

"Bah!" said Scrooge. "Humbug!"

He had so heated himself with rapid walking in the fog and frost, this nephew of Scrooge's, that he was all in a glow; his face was ruddy and handsome; his eyes sparkled, and his breath smoked again.

"Christmas a humbug, uncle!" said Scrooge's nephew. "You don't mean that, I am sure?"

"I do," said Scrooge. "Merry Christmas! What

right have you to be merry? What reason have you to be merry? You're poor enough."

"Come, then," returned the nephew gaily. "What right have you to be dismal? What reason have you to be morose? You're rich enough."

Scrooge, having no better answer ready on the spur of the moment, said "Bah!" again; and followed it up with "Humbug!"

"Don't be cross, uncle!" said the nephew.

"What else can I be," returned the uncle, "when I live in such a world of fools as this? Merry Christmas! Out upon Merry Christmas! What's Christmas-time to you but a time for paying bills without money; a time for finding yourself a year older, and not an hour richer; a time for balancing your books, and having every item in 'em through a round dozen of months presented dead against you? If I could work my will," said Scrooge indignantly, "every idiot who goes about with 'Merry Christmas' on his lips should be boiled with his own pudding, and buried with a stake of holly through his heart. He should!"

"Uncle!" pleaded the nephew.

"Nephew!" returned the uncle sternly, "keep Christmas in your own way, and let me keep it in mine."

"Keep it!" repeated Scrooge's nephew. "But you don't keep it."

"Let me leave it alone, then," said Scrooge.

6

"Much good may it do you! Much good it has ever done you!"

"There are many things from which I might have derived good by which I have not profited, I dare say," returned the nephew, "Christmas among the rest. But I am sure I have always thought of Christmas-time, when it has come round—apart from the veneration due to its sacred name and origin, if anything belonging to it can be apart from that—as a good time; a kind, forgiving, charitable, pleasant time; the only time I know of, in the long calendar of the year, when men and women seem by one consent to open their shut-up hearts freely, and to think of people below them as if they really were fellow-passengers to the grave, and not another race of creatures bound on other journeys. And therefore, uncle, though it has never put a scrap of gold or silver in my pocket, I believe that it *has* done me good, and *will* do me good; and I say, God bless it!"

The clerk in the tank involuntarily applauded. Becoming immediately sensible of the impropriety, he poked the fire, and extinguished the last frail spark forever.

"Let me hear another sound from *you*," said Scrooge, "and you'll keep your Christmas by losing your situation! You're quite a powerful speaker, sir," he added, turning to his nephew. "I wonder you don't go into Parliament."

"Don't be angry, uncle. Come! Dine with us tomorrow."

Scrooge said that he would see him——Yes, indeed, he did. He went the whole length of the expression, and said that he would see him in that extremity first.

"But why?" cried Scrooge's nephew. "Why?"

"Why did you get married?" said Scrooge.

"Because I fell in love."

"Because you fell in love!" growled Scrooge, as if that were the only one thing in the world more ridiculous than a Merry Christmas. "Good afternoon!"

"Nay, uncle, but you never came to see me before that happened. Why give it as a reason for not coming now?"

"Good afternoon," said Scrooge.

"I want nothing from you; I ask nothing of you; why cannot we be friends?"

"Good afternoon!" said Scrooge.

"I am sorry, with all my heart, to find you so resolute. We have never had any quarrel, to which I have been a party. But I have made the trial in homage to Christmas, and I'll keep my Christmas humor to the last. So a Merry Christmas, uncle!"

"Good afternoon," said Scrooge.

"And a Happy New Year!"

"Good afternoon!" said Scrooge.

His nephew left the room without an angry word, notwithstanding. He stopped at the outer door to bestow the greetings of the season on the clerk, who, cold as he was, was warmer than Scrooge, for he returned them cordially.

"There's another fellow," muttered Scrooge, who overheard him; "my clerk, with fifteen shillings a week, and a wife and family, talking about a Merry Christmas. I'll retire to Bedlam."

This lunatic, in letting Scrooge's nephew out, had let two other people in. They were portly gentlemen, pleasant to behold, and now stood with their hats off, in Scrooge's office. They had books and papers in their hands, and bowed to him.

"Scrooge and Marley's, I believe," said one of the gentlemen, referring to his list. "Have I the pleasure of addressing Mr. Scrooge, or Mr. Marley?"

"Mr. Marley has been dead these seven years," Scrooge replied. "He died seven years ago, this very night."

"We have no doubt his liberality is well represented by his surviving partner," said the gentleman, presenting his credentials.

It certainly was; for they had been two kindred spirits. At the ominous word "liberality," Scrooge frowned, and shook his head, and handed the credentials back.

"At this festive season of the year, Mr. Scrooge," said the gentleman, taking up a pen, "it is more than usually desirable that we should make some slight provision for the poor and destitute who suffer greatly at the present time. Many thousands are in want of common necessaries; hundreds of thousands are in want of common comforts, sir."

"Are there no prisons?" asked Scrooge.

"Plenty of prisons," said the gentleman, laying down the pen again.

"And the Union workhouses?" demanded Scrooge. "Are they still in operation?"

"They are. Still," returned the gentleman, "I wish I could say they were not."

"The Treadmill and the Poor Law are in full vigor, then?" said Scrooge.

"Both very busy, sir."

"Oh! I was afraid from what you said at first, that something had occurred to stop them in their useful course," said Scrooge. "I'm very glad to hear it."

"Under the impression that they scarcely furnish Christian cheer of mind or body to the multitude," returned the gentleman, "a few of us are endeavoring to raise a fund to buy the poor some meat and drink, and means of warmth. We choose this time, because it is a time, of all others, when Want is keenly felt, and Abundance rejoices. What shall I put you down for?"

"Nothing!" Scrooge replied.

"You wish to be anonymous?"

"I wish to be left alone," said Scrooge. "Since you ask me what I wish, gentlemen, that is my answer. I don't make merry myself at Christmas, and I can't afford to make idle people merry. I help to support the establishments I have mentioned—they cost enough; and those who are badly off must go there."

"Many can't go there; and many would rather die."

"If they would rather die," said Scrooge, "they had better do it, and decrease the surplus population. Besides—excuse me—I don't know that."

"But you might know it," observed the gentleman.

"It's not my business," Scrooge returned. "It's enough for a man to understand his own business, and not to interfere with other people's. Mine occupies me constantly. Good afternoon, gentlemen!"

Seeing clearly that it would be useless to pursue their point, the gentlemen withdrew. Scrooge resumed his labors with an improved opinion of himself, and in a more facetious temper than was usual with him.

Meanwhile the fog and darkness thickened so that people ran about with flaring links, proffering their services to go before horses in carriages, and conduct them on their way. The ancient tower of a church, whose gruff old bell was always peeping slyly down at Scrooge out of a Gothic window in the wall, became invisible, and struck the hours and quarters in the clouds, with tremulous vibrations afterward, as if its teeth were chattering in its frozen head up there. The cold became intense. In the main street, at the corner of the court, some laborers were repairing the gas pipes, and had lighted a great fire in a brazier, round which a party of ragged men and boys were gathered, warming their hands and winking their eyes before the blaze, in rapture. The water-plug being left in solitude, its overflowings suddenly congealed, and turned to misanthropic ice. The brightness of the shops, where holly sprigs and berries crackled in the lamp heat of the windows, made pale faces ruddy as they passed. Poulterers' and grocers' trades became a splendid joke; a glorious pageant, with which it was next to impossible to believe that such dull principles as bargain and sale had anything to do. The Lord Mayor, in the stronghold of the mighty Mansion House, gave orders to his fifty cooks and butlers to keep Christmas as a Lord Mayor's household should; and even the little tailor, whom he had fined five shillings on the previous Monday for being drunk and bloodthirsty in the streets, stirred up tomorrow's pudding in his garret, while his lean wife and baby sallied out to buy the beef.

Foggier yet, and colder! Piercing, searching, biting cold. If the good Saint Dunstan had but nipped the Evil Spirit's nose with a touch of such weather as that, instead of using his familiar weapons, then, indeed, he would have roared to lusty purpose. The owner of one scant young nose, gnawed and mumbled by the hungry cold as bones are gnawed by dogs, stooped down at Scrooge's keyhole to regale him with a Christmas carol; but at the first sound of

'God rest you, merry gentleman!
May nothing you dismay!'

Scrooge seized the ruler with such energy of action, that the singer fled in terror, leaving the keyhole to the fog and even more congenial frost.

At length the hour of shutting up the counting-house arrived. With an ill will Scrooge dismounted from his stool, and tacitly admitted the fact to the expectant clerk in the tank, who instantly snuffed his candle out, and put on his hat.

"You'll want all day tomorrow, I suppose?" said Scrooge.

"If quite convenient, sir."

"It's not convenient," said Scrooge, "and it's not fair. If I was to stop half a crown for it, you'd think yourself ill used, I'll be bound?"

The clerk smiled faintly.

"And yet," said Scrooge, "you don't think *me* ill used when I pay a day's wages for no work."

The clerk observed that it was only once a year.

"A poor excuse for picking a man's pocket every

twenty-fifth of December!" said Scrooge, buttoning his greatcoat to the chin. "But I suppose you must have the whole day. Be here all the earlier next morning."

The clerk promised that he would; and Scrooge walked out with a growl. The office was closed in a twinkling, and the clerk, with the long ends of his white comforter dangling below his waist (for he boasted no greatcoat), went down a slide on Cornhill, at the end of a lane of boys, twenty times, in honor of its being Christmas Eve, and then ran home to Camden Town, as hard as he could pelt, to play at blindman's buff.

Scrooge took his melancholy dinner in his usual melancholy tavern; and having read all the newspapers, and beguiled the rest of the evening with his banker's book, went home to bed. He lived in chambers which had once belonged to his deceased partner. They were a gloomy suite of rooms, in a lowering pile of building up a yard, where it had so little business to be, that one could scarcely help fancying it must have run there when it was a young house, playing at hide-and-seek with other houses, and have forgotten the way out again. It was old enough now, and dreary enough, for nobody lived in it but Scrooge, the other rooms being all let out as offices. The yard was so dark that even Scrooge, who knew its every stone, was fain to grope with his hands. The fog and frost so hung about the black old gateway of the house, that it seemed as if the Genius of the Weather sat in mournful meditation on the threshold.

Now it is a fact that there was nothing at all particular about the knocker on the door, except that it was very large. It is also a fact that Scrooge had seen it, night and morning, during his whole residence in that place; also that Scrooge had as little of what is called fancy about him as any man in the City of London, even including—which is a bold word—the corporation, aldermen, and livery. Let it also be borne in mind that Scrooge had not bestowed one thought on Marley, since his last mention of his seven-years-dead partner that afternoon. And then let any man explain to me, if he can, how it happened that Scrooge, having his key in the lock of the door, saw in the knocker, without its undergoing any intermediate process of change—not a knocker, but Marley's face.

Marley's face. It was not in impenetrable shadow, as the other objects in the yard were, but had a dismal light about it, like a bad lobster in a dark cellar. It was not angry or ferocious, but looked at Scrooge as Marley used to look: with ghostly spectacles turned up on its ghostly forehead. The hair was curiously stirred, as if by breath or hot air; and though the eyes were wide open, they were perfectly motionless. That, and its livid color, made it horrible; but its horror seemed to be in spite of the face, and beyond its control, rather than a part of its own expression.

As Scrooge looked fixedly at this phenomenon it was a knocker again.

To say that he was not startled, or that his blood was not conscious of a terrible sensation to which it had been a stranger from infancy, would be untrue. But he put his hand upon the key he had relinquished, turned it sturdily, walked in, and lighted his candle.

He *did* pause, with a moment's irresolution, before he shut the door; and he *did* look cautiously behind it first, as if he half expected to be terrified with the sight of Marley's pigtail sticking out into the hall. But there was nothing on the back of the door, except the screws and nuts that held the knocker on, so he said, "Pooh, pooh!" and closed it with a bang.

The sound resounded through the house like thunder. Every room above, and every cask in the wine-merchant's cellars below, appeared to have a separate peal of echoes of its own. Scrooge was not a man to be frightened by echoes. He fastened the door, and walked across the hall, and up the stairs, slowly, too, trimming his candle as he went.

You may talk vaguely about driving a coach and six up a good old flight of stairs, or through a bad young Act of Parliament; but I mean to say you might have got a hearse up that staircase, and taken it broadwise, the splinter-bar toward the wall, and the door toward the balustrades, and done it easy. There was plenty of width for that, and room to spare; which is perhaps the reason why Scrooge thought he saw a locomotive hearse going on before him in the gloom. Half a dozen gas lamps out of the street wouldn't have lighted the entry too well, so you may suppose that it was pretty dark with Scrooge's dip.

Up Scrooge went, not caring a button for that. Darkness is cheap, and Scrooge liked it. But before he shut his heavy door, he walked through his rooms to see that all was right. He had just enough recollection of the face to desire to do that.

Sitting room, bedroom, lumber room. All as they should be. Nobody under the table, nobody under the sofa; a small fire in the grate; spoon and basin ready; and the little saucepan of gruel (Scrooge had a cold in his head) upon the hob. Nobody under the bed; nobody in the closet; nobody in his dressing gown, which was hanging up in a suspicious attitude against the wall. Lumber room as usual. Old fireguard, old shoes, two fish-baskets, washing-stand on three legs, and a poker.

Quite satisfied, he closed his door, and locked himself in; double-locked himself in, which was not his custom. Thus secured against surprise, he took off his cravat, put on his dressing gown and slippers, and his nightcap, and sat down before the fire to take his gruel.

It was a very low fire indeed; nothing on such a bitter night. He was obliged to sit close to it, and brood over it, before he could extract the least sensation of warmth from such a handful of fuel. The fireplace was an old one, built by some Dutch merchant long ago, and paved all round with quaint Dutch tiles, designed to illustrate the Scriptures. There were Cains and Abels, Pharaoh's daughters, Queens of Sheba, angelic messengers descending through the air on clouds like featherbeds, Abrahams, Belshazzars, Apostles putting off to sea in butter-boats, hundreds of figures to attract his thoughts; and yet that face of Marley, seven years dead, came like the ancient Prophet's rod, and swallowed up the whole. If each smooth tile had been a blank at first, with power to shape some picture on its surface from the disjointed fragments of his thoughts, there would have been a copy of old Marley's head on every one.

"Humbug!" said Scrooge; and walked across the room.

After several turns, he sat down again. As he threw his head back in the chair, his glance happened to rest upon a bell, a disused bell, that hung in the room, and communicated, for some purpose now forgotten, with a chamber in the highest story of the building. It was with great astonishment, and with a strange, inexplicable dread, that, as he looked, he saw this bell begin to swing. It swung so softly in the outset that it scarcely made a sound; but soon it rang out loudly, and so did every bell in the house.

This might have lasted a half a minute, or a minute, but it seemed an hour. The bells ceased, as they had begun, together. They were succeeded by a clanking noise, deep down below; as if some person were dragging a heavy chain over the casks in the wine merchant's cellar. Scrooge then remembered to have heard that ghosts in haunted houses were described as dragging chains.

The cellar door flew open with a booming sound, and then he heard the noise, much louder, on the floors below; then coming up the stairs; then coming straight toward his door.

"It's humbug still!" said Scrooge. "I won't believe it!"

His color changed, though, when, without a pause, it came on through the heavy door, and passed into the room before his eyes. Upon its coming in, the dying flame leaped up, as though it cried, "I know him! Marley's Ghost!" and fell again.

The same face, the very same. Marley, in his pigtail, usual waistcoat, tights and boots; the tassels on the latter bristling like his pigtail, and his coat-skirts, and the hair upon his head. The chain he drew was clasped about his middle. It was long, and wound about him like a tail; and it was made (for Scrooge observed it closely) of cash-boxes, keys, padlocks, ledgers, deeds, and heavy purses wrought in steel. His body was transparent; so that Scrooge, observing him, and looking through his waistcoat, could see the two buttons on his coat behind.

Scrooge had often heard it said that Marley had no bowels, but he had never believed it until now.

No, nor did he believe it even now. Though he looked the phantom through and through, and saw it standing before him; though he felt the chilling influence of its death-cold eyes, and marked the very texture of the folded kerchief bound about its head and chin, which wrapper he had not observed before, he was still incredulous, and fought against his senses.

"How now!" said Scrooge, caustic and cold as ever. "What do you want with me?"

"Much!"—Marley's voice, no doubt about it.

"Who are you?"

"Ask me who I *was*."

"Who *were* you, then?" said Scrooge, raising his voice. "You're particular, for a shade." He was going to say, "*to* a shade," but substituted this, as more appropriate.

"In life I was your partner, Jacob Marley."

"Can you—can you sit down?" asked Scrooge, looking doubtfully at him.

"I can."

"Do it, then."

Scrooge asked the question, because he didn't

know whether a ghost so transparent might find himself in a condition to take a chair; and felt in the event of its being impossible, it might involve the necessity of an embarrassing explanation. But the Ghost sat down on the opposite side of the fireplace, as if he were quite used to it.

"You don't believe in me," observed the Ghost.

"I don't," said Scrooge.

"What evidence would you have of my reality beyond that of your own senses?"

"I don't know," said Scrooge.

"Why do you doubt your senses?"

"Because," said Scrooge, "a little thing affects them. A slight disorder of the stomach makes them cheats. You may be an undigested bit of beef, a blot of mustard, a crumb of cheese, a fragment of an underdone potato. There's more of gravy than of grave about you, whatever you are!"

Scrooge was not much in the habit of cracking jokes, nor did he feel, in his heart, by any means waggish then. The truth is, that he tried to be smart, as a means of distracting his own attention, and keeping down his terror, for the specter's voice disturbed the very marrow in his bones.

To sit staring at those fixed glazed eyes in silence, for a moment, would play, Scrooge felt, the very deuce with him. There was something very awful, too, in the specter's being provided with an infernal atmosphere of his own. Scrooge could not feel it himself, but this was clearly the

case; for though the Ghost sat perfectly motionless, his hair, and skirts, and tassels were still
agitated as by the hot vapor from an oven.

"You see this toothpick?" said Scrooge,
returning quickly to the charge, for the reason just
assigned; and wishing, though it were only for a
second, to divert the vision's stony gaze from
himself.

"I do," replied the Ghost.

"You are not looking at it," said Scrooge.

"But I see it," said the Ghost, "notwithstanding."

"Well!" returned Scrooge, "I have but to
swallow this, and be for the rest of my days
persecuted by a legion of goblins, all my own
creation. Humbug, I tell you; humbug!"

At this the spirit raised a frightful cry, and
shook his chain with such a dismal and appalling
noise, that Scrooge held on tight to his chair, to
save himself from falling in a swoon. But how
much greater was his horror when, the phantom
taking off the bandage round his head, as if it were
too warm to wear indoors, his lower jaw dropped
down upon his breast!

Scrooge fell upon his knees, and clasped his
hands before his face.

"Mercy!" he said. "Dreadful apparition, why do
you trouble me?"

"Man of the worldly mind!" replied the Ghost,
"do you believe in me or not?"

"I do," said Scrooge. "I must. But why do spirits walk the earth, and why do they come to me?"

"It is required of every man," the Ghost returned, "that the spirit within him should walk abroad among his fellow-men, and travel far and wide; and if that spirit goes not forth in life, it is condemned to do so after death. It is doomed to wander through the world—oh, woe is me!—and witness what it cannot share, but might have shared on earth, and turned to happiness!"

Again, the specter raised a cry, and shook his chain and wrung his shadowy hands.

"You are fettered," said Scrooge trembling. "Tell me why?"

"I wear the chain I forged in life," replied the Ghost. "I made it link by link, and yard by yard; I girded it on of my own free will, and of my own free will I wore it. Is its pattern strange to *you*?"

Scrooge trembled more and more.

"Or would you know," pursued the Ghost, "the weight and length of the strong coil you bear yourself? It was full as heavy and as long as this, seven Christmas Eves ago. You have labored on it, since. It is a ponderous chain!"

Scrooge glanced about him on the floor, in the expectation of finding himself surrounded by some fifty or sixty fathoms of iron cable; but he could see nothing.

"Jacob!" he said imploringly. "Old Jacob

Marley, tell me more! Speak comfort to me, Jacob!"

"I have none to give," the Ghost replied. "It comes from other regions, Ebenezer Scrooge, and is conveyed by other ministers, to other kinds of men. Nor can I tell you what I would. A very little more is all permitted to me. I cannot rest, I cannot stay, I cannot linger anywhere. My spirit never walked beyond our counting-house—mark me!—in life my spirit never roved beyond the narrow limits of our money-changing hole; and weary journeys lie before me!"

It was a habit with Scrooge, whenever he became thoughtful, to put his hands in his breeches' pockets. Pondering on what the Ghost had said, he did so now, but without lifting up his eyes, or getting off his knees.

"You must have been very slow about it, Jacob," Scrooge observed in a businesslike manner, though with humility and deference.

"Slow!" the Ghost repeated.

"Seven years dead," mused Scrooge. "And traveling all the time?"

"The whole time," said the Ghost. "No rest, no peace. Incessant torture of remorse."

"You travel fast?" said Scrooge.

"On the wings of the wind," replied the Ghost.

"You must have got over a great quantity of ground in seven years," said Scrooge.

The Ghost, on hearing this, set up another cry,

and clanked his chain so hideously in the dead silence of the night, that the Ward would have been justified in indicating it for a nuisance.

"Oh! captive, bound and double-ironed," cried the phantom, "not to know that ages of incessant labor, by immortal creatures, for this earth, must pass into eternity before the good of which it is susceptible is all developed! Not to know that any Christian spirit working kindly in its little sphere, whatever it may be, will find its mortal life too short for its vast means of usefulness! Not to know that no space or regret can make amends for one life's opportunities misused! Yet such was I! Oh! such was I!"

"But you were always a good man of business, Jacob," faltered Scrooge, who now began to apply this to himself.

"Business!" cried the Ghost, wringing his hands again. "Mankind was my business. The common welfare was my business; charity, mercy, forbearance, and benevolence were all my business. The dealings of my trade were but a drop of water in the comprehensive ocean of my business!"

He held up his chain at arm's-length, as if that were the cause of all his unavailing grief, and flung it heavily upon the ground again.

"At this time of the rolling year," the specter said, "I suffer most. Why did I walk through crowds of fellow-beings with my eyes turned down, and never raise them to that blessed Star which led the Wise Men to a poor abode? Were there no poor homes to which its light would have conducted *me*?"

Scrooge was very much dismayed to hear the specter going on at this rate, and began to quake exceedingly.

"Hear me!" cried the Ghost. "My time is nearly gone."

"I will," said Scrooge. "But don't be hard upon me! Don't be flowery, Jacob! Pray!"

"How it is that I appear before you in a shape that you can see, I may not tell. I have sat invisible beside you many and many a day."

It was not an agreeable idea. Scrooge shivered, and wiped the perspiration from his brow.

"That is no light part of my penance," pursued the Ghost. "I am here tonight to warn you, that you have yet a chance and hope of escaping my fate. A chance and hope of my procuring, Ebenezer."

"You were always a good friend to me," said Scrooge. "Thankee!"

"You will be haunted," resumed the Ghost, "by Three Spirits."

Scrooge's countenance fell almost as low as the Ghost's had done.

"Is that the chance and hope you mentioned, Jacob?" he demanded in a faltering voice.

"It is."

"I—I think I'd rather not," said Scrooge.

"Without their visits," said the Ghost, "you cannot hope to shun the path I tread. Expect the first tomorrow, when the bell tolls One."

"Couldn't I take 'em all at once, and have it over, Jacob?" hinted Scrooge.

"Expect the second on the next night at the same hour. The third, upon the next night when the last stroke of Twelve has ceased to vibrate. Look to see me no more; and look that, for your own sake, you remember what has passed between us!"

When he had said these words, the specter took his wrapper from the table, and bound it round his head, as before. Scrooge knew this, by the smart sound his teeth made when the jaws were brought together by the bandage. He ventured to raise his eyes again, and found his supernatural visitor confronting him in an erect attitude, with his chain wound over and about his arm.

The apparition walked backward from him; and at every step he took, the window raised itself a little, so that when the specter reached it, it was wide open. He beckoned Scrooge to approach, which he did. When they were within two paces of each other, Marley's Ghost held up his hand, warning him to come no nearer. Scrooge stopped.

Not so much in obedience, as in surprise and fear; for on the raising of the hand he became sensible of confused noises in the air; incoherent sounds of lamentation and regret; wailings inexpressibly sorrowful and self-accusatory. The specter, after listening for a moment, joined in the mournful dirge; and floated out upon the bleak, dark night.

Scrooge followed to the window, desperate in his curiosity. He looked out.

The air was filled with phantoms, wandering hither and thither in restless haste, and moaning as they went. Every one of them wore chains like Marley's Ghost; some few (they might be guilty governments) were linked together; none were free. Many had been personally known to Scrooge in their lives. He had been quite familiar with one old ghost, in a white waistcoat, with a monstrous iron safe attached to his ankle, who cried piteously at being unable to assist a wretched woman with an infant, whom he saw below, upon a doorstep. The misery with them all was, clearly, that they sought to interfere, for good, in human matters, and had lost the power forever.

Whether these creatures faded into mist, or mist enshrouded them, he could not tell. But they and their spirit voices faded together; and the night became as it had been when he walked home.

Scrooge closed the window, and examined the door by which the Ghost had entered. It was double-locked, as he had locked it with his own hands, and the bolts were undisturbed. He tried to say "Humbug!" but stopped at the first syllable.

And being, from the emotion he had undergone, or the fatigues of the day, or his glimpse of the Invisible World, or the dull conversation of the Ghost, or the lateness of the hour, much in need of repose, went straight to bed, without undressing, and fell asleep on the instant.

Stave Two
The First of the Three Spirits

When Scrooge awoke it was so dark, that, looking out of bed, he could scarcely distinguish the transparent window from the opaque walls of his chamber. He was endeavoring to pierce the darkness with his ferret eyes, when the chimes of a neighboring church struck the four quarters. So he listened for the hour.

To his great astonishment the heavy bell went on from six to seven, and from seven to eight, and regularly up to twelve; then stopped. Twelve! It was past two when he went to bed. The clock was wrong. An icicle must have got into the works. Twelve!

He touched the spring of his repeater, to correct this most preposterous clock. Its rapid little pulse beat twelve; and stopped.

"Why, it isn't possible," said Scrooge, "that I can have slept through a whole day and far into another night. It isn't possible that anything has happened to the sun, and this is twelve at noon!"

The idea being an alarming one, he scrambled out of bed, and groped his way to the window. He was obliged to rub the frost off with the sleeve of his dressing gown before he could see anything; and could see very little then. All he could make out was, that it was still very foggy and extremely cold, and that there was no noise of people running to and fro, and making a great stir, as there unquestionably would have been if night had beaten off bright day, and taken possession of the world. This was a great relief, because "Three days after sight of this First of Exchange pay to Mr. Ebenezer Scrooge or his order," and so forth, would have become a mere United States security if there were no days to count by.

Scrooge went to bed again, and thought, and thought, and thought it over and over, and could make nothing of it. The more he thought, the more perplexed he was; and the more he endeavored not to think, the more he thought.

Marley's Ghost bothered him exceedingly. Every time he resolved within himself, after mature inquiry, that it was all a dream, his mind flew back again, like a strong spring released, to its first position, and presented the same problem to be worked all through, "Was it a dream or not?"

Scrooge lay in this state until the chime had gone three quarters more, when he remembered, on a sudden, that the Ghost had warned him of a visitation when the bell tolled One. He resolved to lie awake until the hour was passed; and, considering that he could no more go to sleep than go to Heaven, this was, perhaps, the wisest resolution in his power.

The quarter was so long, that he was more than once convinced he must have sunk into a doze unconsciously, and missed the clock. At length it broke upon his listening ear.

"Ding, dong!"

"A quarter past," said Scrooge, counting.

"Ding, dong!"

"Half past," said Scrooge.

"Ding, dong!"

"A quarter to it," said Scrooge.

"Ding, dong!"

"The hour itself," said Scrooge triumphantly, "and nothing else!"

He spoke before the hour bell sounded, which it now did with a deep, dull, hollow, melancholy ONE. Lights flashed up in the room upon the instant, and the curtains of his bed were drawn.

The curtains of his bed were drawn aside, I tell you, by a hand. Not the curtains at his feet, nor the curtains at his back, but those to which his face was addressed. The curtains of his bed were drawn aside; and Scrooge, starting up into a half recumbent attitude, found himself face to face with the unearthly visitor who drew them: as close to it as I am now to you, and I am standing in the spirit at your elbow.

It was a strange figure—like a child; yet not so like a child as like an old man, viewed through some supernatural medium, which gave him the appearance of having receded from the view, and being diminished to a child's proportions. Its hair, which hung about its neck and down its back, was white, as if with age; and yet the face had not a wrinkle in it, and the tenderest bloom was on the skin. The arms were very long and muscular; the hands the same, as if its hold were of uncommon strength. Its legs and feet, most delicately formed, were, like those upper members, bare. It wore a tunic of the purest white; and round its waist was bound a lustrous belt, the sheen of which was beautiful. It held a branch of fresh, green holly in its hand; and, in singular contradiction to that wintry emblem, had its dress trimmed with summer flowers. But the strangest thing about it was, that from the crown of its head there sprung a bright, clear jet of light, by which all this was visible; and which was doubtless the occasion of its using, in its duller moments, a great extinguisher for a cap, which it now held under its arm.

Even this, though, when Scrooge looked at it with increasing steadiness, was *not* its strangest quality. For as its belt sparkled and glittered now in one part and now in another, and what was light one instant at another time was dark, so the figure itself fluctuated in its distinctness: being now a thing with one arm, now with one leg, now with twenty legs, now a pair of legs without a head, now a head without a body; of which dissolving parts no outline would be visible in the dense gloom wherein they melted away. And, in the very wonder of this, it would be itself again, distinct and clear as ever.

"Are you the Spirit, sir, whose coming was foretold to me?" asked Scrooge.

"I am!"

The voice was soft and gentle. Singularly low, as if instead of being so close beside him, it were at a distance.

"Who, and what are you?" Scrooge demanded.

"I am the Ghost of Christmas Past."

"Long Past?" inquired Scrooge, observant of its dwarfish stature.

"No. Your past."

Perhaps Scrooge could not have told anybody why, if anybody could have asked him, but he had a special desire to see the Spirit in his cap, and begged him to be covered.

"What!" exclaimed the Ghost, "would you so soon put out, with worldly hands, the light I give? Is it not enough that you are of those whose passions made this cap, and force me through whole trains of years to wear it low upon my brow?''

Scrooge reverently disclaimed all intention to offend or any knowledge of having wilfully ''bonneted'' the Spirit at any period of his life. He then made bold to inquire what business brought him there.

''Your welfare!'' said the Ghost.

Scrooge expressed himself as much obliged, but could not help thinking that a night of unbroken rest would have been more conducive to that end. The Spirit must have heard him thinking, for it said immediately:

''Your reclamation, then. Take heed!''

It put out its strong hand as it spoke, and clasped him gently by the arm.

''Rise, and walk with me!''

It would have been in vain for Scrooge to plead that the weather and the hour were not adapted to pedestrian purposes; that his bed was warm, and the thermometer a long way below freezing; that he was clad but lightly in his slippers, dressing gown, and nightcap; and that he had a cold upon him at that time. The grasp, though gentle as a woman's hand, was not to be resisted. He rose; but finding that the Spirit made toward the window, clasped its robe in supplication.

''I am a mortal,'' Scrooge remonstrated, ''and liable to fall.''

''Bear but a touch of my hand *there*,'' said the

Spirit laying it upon his heart, "and you shall be upheld in more than this!"

As the words were spoken, they passed through the wall, and stood upon an open country road, with fields on either hand. The city had entirely vanished. Not a vestige of it was to be seen. The darkness and the mist had vanished with it, for it was a clear, cold, winter day, with snow upon the ground.

"Good Heaven!" said Scrooge, clasping his hands together, as he looked about him. "I was bred in this place. I was a boy here!"

The Spirit gazed upon him mildly. Its gentle touch, though it had been light and instantaneous, appeared still present to the old man's sense of feeling. He was conscious of a thousand odors floating in the air, each one connected with a thousand thoughts, and hopes, and joys, and cares long, long forgotten!

"Your lip is trembling," said the Ghost. "And what is that upon your cheek?"

Scrooge muttered, with an unusual catching in his voice, that it was a pimple, and begged the Ghost to lead him to where he would.

"You recollect the way?" inquired the Spirit.

"Remember it!" cried Scrooge with fervor, "I could walk it blindfolded."

"Strange to have forgotten it for so many years!" observed the Ghost. "Let us go on."

They walked along the road, Scrooge recognizing every gate, and post, and tree; until a little market town appeared in the distance, with its bridge, its church, and winding river. Some shaggy ponies now were seen trotting toward them, with boys upon their backs, who called to other boys in country gigs and carts, driven by farmers. All these boys were in great spirits, and shouted to each other, until the broad fields were so full of merry music that the crisp air laughed to hear it.

"These are but shadows of the things that have been," said the Ghost. "They have no consciousness of us."

The jocund travelers came on; and as they came, Scrooge knew and named them every one. Why was he rejoiced beyond all bounds to see them? Why did his cold eye glisten, and his heart leap up as they went past? Why was he filled with gladness when he heard them give each other Merry Christmas, as they parted at crossroads and byways, for their several homes? What was Merry Christmas to Scrooge? Out upon Merry Christmas! What good had it ever done to him?

"The school is not quite deserted," said the Ghost. "A solitary child, neglected by his friends, is left there still."

Scrooge said he knew it. And he sobbed.

They left the high road, by a well-remembered lane, and soon approached a mansion of dull red brick, with a little weather cock-surmounted cupola, on the roof, and a bell hanging in it. It was a large house, but one of broken fortunes; for the spacious offices were little used, their walls were damp and mossy, their windows broken, and their gates decayed. Fowls clucked and strutted in the stables, and the coach-houses and sheds were overrun with grass. Nor was it more retentive of its ancient state, within; for entering the dreary hall, and glancing through the open doors of many rooms, they found them poorly furnished, cold, and vast. There was an earthy savor in the air, a chilly bareness in the place, which associated itself somehow with too much getting up by candle-light, and not too much to eat.

They went, the Ghost and Scrooge, across the hall, to a door at the back of the house. It opened before them, and disclosed a long, bare, melancholy room, made barer still by lines of plain deal forms and desks. At one of these a lonely boy was reading near a feeble fire; and Scrooge sat down upon a form, and wept to see his poor forgotten self as he used to be.

Not a latent echo in the house, not a squeak and scuffle from the mice behind the paneling, not a drip from the half-thawed waterspout in the dull yard behind, not a sigh among the leafless boughs of one despondent poplar, not the idle swinging of an empty storehouse door, no, not a clicking in the fire, but fell upon the heart of Scrooge with softening influence, and gave a freer passage to his tears.

The Spirit touched him on the arm, and pointed to his younger self, intent upon his reading. Suddenly a man, in foreign garments, wonderfully real and distinct to look at, stood outside the window, with an ax stuck in his belt, and leading by the bridle an ass laden with wood.

"Why, it's Ali Baba!" Scrooge exclaimed in ecstasy. "It's dear old honest Ali Baba! Yes, yes, I know! One Christmas-time, when yonder solitary child was left here all alone, he *did* come, for the first time, just like that. Poor boy! And Valentine," said Scrooge, "and his wild brother Orson; there they go! And what's his name, who was put down in his drawers, asleep, at the Gate of Damascus; don't you see him? And the Sultan's Groom turned upside down by the Genii; there he is upon his head! Serve him right! I'm glad of it. What business had *he* to be married to the Princess?"

To hear Scrooge expending all the earnestness of his nature on such subjects, in a most extraordinary voice between laughing and crying, and to see his heightened and excited face, would have been a surprise to his business friends in the City, indeed.

"There's the Parrot!" cried Scrooge. "Green body and yellow tail, with a thing like a lettuce growing out of the top of his head; there he is! Poor Robin Crusoe, he called him, when he came home again, after sailing around the island. 'Poor Robin Crusoe, where have you been, Robin Crusoe?' The man thought he was dreaming, but he wasn't. It was the Parrot, you know. There goes Friday, running for his life to the little creek! Halloa! Hoop! Halloa!"

Then, with a rapidity of transition very foreign to his usual character, he said, in pity for his former self, "Poor boy!" and cried again.

"I wish," Scrooge muttered, putting his hand in his pocket, and looking about him, after drying his eyes with his cuff, "but it's too late now."

"What is the matter?" asked the Spirit.

"Nothing," said Scrooge, "nothing. There was a boy singing a Christmas carol at my door last night. I should like to have given him something, that's all."

The Ghost smiled thoughtfully, and waved its hand, saying, as it did so, "Let us see another Christmas!"

Scrooge's former self grew larger at the words, and the room became a little darker and dirty. The panels shrunk, the windows cracked; fragments of plaster fell out of the ceiling, and the naked laths were shown instead; but how all this was brought about, Scrooge knew no more than you do. He only knew that it was quite correct; that everything had happened so; that there he was, alone again, when all the other boys had gone home for the jolly holidays.

He was not reading now, but walking up and down despairingly. Scrooge looked at the Ghost, and, with a mournful shaking of his head, glanced anxiously toward the door.

It opened, and a little girl, much younger than the boy, came darting in, and, putting her arms about his neck, and often kissing him, addressed him as her "dear, dear, brother."

"I have come to bring you home, dear brother!" said the child, clapping her tiny hands, and bending down to laugh. "To bring you home, home, home!"

"Home, little Fan?" returned the boy.

"Yes!" said the child, brimful of glee. "Home, for good and all. Home, forever and ever. Father is so much kinder than he used to be, that home's like Heaven! He spoke so gently to me one dear night when I was going to bed that I was not afraid to ask him once more if you might come home; and he said Yes, you should; and sent me in a coach to bring you. And you're to be a man!" said the child, opening her eyes, "and are never to come back here; but first, we're to be together all the Christmas long, and have the merriest time in all the world."

"You are quite a woman, little Fan!" exclaimed the boy.

She clapped her hands and laughed, and tried to

touch his head; but, being too little, laughed again, and stood on tiptoe to embrace him. Then she began to drag him, in her childish eagerness, toward the door; and he, nothing loath to go, accompanied her.

A terrible voice in the hall cried, "Bring down Master Scrooge's box, there!" and in the hall appeared the schoolmaster himself, who glared on Master Scrooge with a ferocious condescension, and threw him into a dreadful state of mind by shaking hands with him. He then conveyed him and his sister into the veriest old well of a shivering best parlor that ever was seen, where the maps upon the wall, and the celestial and terrestrial globes in the windows, were waxy with cold. Here he produced a decanter of curiously light wine, and a block of curiously heavy cake, and administered installments of those dainties to the young people; at the same time, sending out a meager servant to offer a glass of "something" to the post-boy, who answered that he thanked the gentleman, but if it was the same tap as he had tasted before, he had rather not. Master Scrooge's trunk being by this time tied onto the top of the chaise, the children bade the schoolmaster good-by right willingly; and, getting into it, drove gaily down the garden sweep, the quick wheels dashing the hoar-frost and snow from off the dark leaves of the evergreens like spray.

"Always a delicate creature, whom a breath

might have withered," said the Ghost. "But she had a large heart!"

"So she had," cried Scrooge. "You're right. I will not gainsay it, Spirit. God forbid!"

"She died a woman," said the Ghost, "and had, as I think, children."

"One child," Scrooge returned.

"True," said the Ghost. "Your nephew!"

Scrooge seemed uneasy in his mind and answered briefly, "Yes."

Although they had but that moment left the school behind them, they were now in the busy thoroughfares of a city, where shadowy passengers passed and repassed, where shadowy carts and coaches battled for the way, and all the strife and tumult of a real city were. It was made plain enough, by the dressing of the shops, that here, too, it was Christmas-time again, but it was evening, and the streets were lighted up.

The Ghost stopped at a certain warehouse door, and asked Scrooge if he knew it.

"Know it!" said Scrooge. "Was I apprenticed here?"

They went in. At sight of an old gentleman in a Welsh wig, sitting behind such a high desk that if he had been two inches taller he must have knocked his head against the ceiling, Scrooge cried in great excitement:

"Why, it's old Fezziwig! Bless his heart; it's Fezziwig alive again!"

Old Fezziwig laid down his pen, and looked up at the clock, which pointed to the hour of seven. He rubbed his hands, adjusted his capacious waistcoat, laughed all over himself, from his shoes to his organ of benevolence and called out, in a comfortable, oily, rich, fat, jovial voice:

"Yo ho, there! Ebenezer! Dick!"

Scrooge's former self, now grown a young man, came briskly in, accompanied by his fellow-'prentice.

"Dick Wilkins, to be sure!" said Scrooge to the Ghost. "Bless me, yes. There he is. He was very much attached to me, was Dick. Poor Dick! Dear, dear!"

"Yo ho, my boys!" said Fezziwig. "No more work tonight. Christmas Eve, Dick. Christmas, Ebenezer! Let's have the shutters up," cried old Fezziwig, with a sharp clap of his hands, "before a man can say Jack Robinson!"

You wouldn't believe how those two fellows went at it! They charged into the street with the shutters—one, two, three—had 'em up in their places—four, five, six—barred 'em and pinned 'em—seven, eight, nine—and came back before you could have got to twelve, panting like racehorses.

"Hilli-ho!" cried old Fezziwig, skipping down from the high desk with wonderful agility. "Clear away, my lads, and let's have lots of room here! Hilli-ho, Dick! Chirrup, Ebenezer!"

Clear away! There was nothing they wouldn't have cleared away, or couldn't have cleared away, with old Fezziwig looking on. It was done in a minute. Every movable was packed off, as if it were dismissed from public life forevermore; the floor was swept and watered, the lamps were trimmed, fuel was heaped upon the fire; and the warehouse was as snug, and warm, and dry, and bright a ballroom as you would desire to see upon a winter's night.

In came a fiddler with a music book, and went up to the loft desk, and made an orchestra of it, and tuned like fifty stomachaches. In came Mrs. Fezziwig, one vast, substantial smile. In came the three Miss Fezziwigs, beaming and lovable. In came the six young followers whose hearts they broke. In came all the young men and women employed in the business. In came the housemaid, with her cousin, the baker. In came the cook, with her brother's particular friend, the milkman. In came the boy from over the way, who was suspected of not having board enough from his master, trying to hide himself behind the girl from next door but one, who was proved to have had her ears pulled by her mistress. In they all came, one after another; some shyly, some boldly, some gracefully, some awkwardly, some pushing, some pulling; in they all came, anyhow and everyhow. Away they all went, twenty couples at once; hands half round and back again the other way; down

45

the middle and up again; round and round in various stages of affectionate grouping; old top couple always turning up in the wrong place; new top couple starting off again, as soon as they got there, all top couples at last, and not a bottom one to help them! When this result was brought about, old Fezziwig, clapping his hands to stop the dance, cried out, "Well done!" and the fiddler plunged his hot face into a pot of porter, especially provided for that purpose. But, scorning rest, upon his reappearance he instantly began again, though there were no dancers yet, as if the other fiddler had been carried home, exhausted, on a shutter, and he were a brand-new man resolved to beat him out of sight, or perish.

There were more dances, and there were forfeits, and more dances, and there was cake, and there was negus, and there was a great piece of cold roast, and there was a great piece of cold boiled, and there were mince-pies, and plenty of beer. But the great effect of the evening came after the roast and boiled, when the fiddler (an artful dog, mind! the sort of man who knew his business better than you or I could have told it him!) struck up "Sir Roger de Coverley." Then old Fezziwig stood out to dance with Mrs. Fezziwig. Top couple, too, with a good stiff piece of work cut out for them; three or four and twenty pair of partners; people who were not to be trifled with; people who *would* dance, and had no notion of walking.

But if they had been twice as many—ah, four times—old Fezziwig would have been a match for them, and so would Mrs. Fezziwig. As to *her*, she was worthy to be his partner in every sense of the term. If that's not high praise, tell me higher, and I'll use it. A positive light appeared to issue from Fezziwig's calves. They shone in every part of the dance like moons. You couldn't have predicted, at any given time, what would become of them next. And when old Fezziwig and Mrs. Fezziwig had gone all through the dance; advance and retire, both hands to your partner, bow and curtsey, corkscrew, thread-the-needle, and back again to your place, Fezziwig "cut"—cut so deftly, that he appeared to wink with his legs, and came upon his feet again without a stagger.

When the clock struck eleven, this domestic ball broke up. Mr. and Mrs. Fezziwig took their stations, one on either side of the door, and shaking hands with every person individually as he or she went out, wished him or her a Merry Christmas. When everybody had retired but the two 'prentices, they did the same to them; and thus the cheerful voices died away, and the lads were left to their beds, which were under a counter in the back shop.

During the whole of this time, Scrooge had acted like a man out of his wits. His heart and soul were in the scene, and with his former self. He corroborated everything, remembered everything, enjoyed everything, and underwent the strangest agitation. It was not until now, when the bright faces of his former self and Dick were turned from them, that he remembered the Ghost, and became conscious that it was looking full upon him, while the light upon its head burned very clear.

"A small matter," said the Ghost, "To make these silly folks so full of gratitude."

"Small!" echoed Scrooge.

The Spirit signed to him to listen to the two apprentices, who were pouring out their hearts in praise of Fezziwig, and, when he had done so, said:

"Why! Is it not? He has spent but a few pounds of your mortal money: three or four, perhaps. Is that so much that he deserves this praise?"

"It isn't that," said Scrooge, heated by the remark, and speaking unconsciously like his former, not his latter self—"it isn't that, Spirit. He has the power to render us happy or unhappy, to make our service light or burdensome, a pleasure or a toil. Say that his power lies in words and looks, in things so slight and insignificant that it is impossible to add and count 'em up; what then? The happiness he gives is quite as great as if it cost a fortune."

He felt the Spirit's glance, and stopped.

"What is the matter?" said the Ghost.

"Nothing particular," said Scrooge.

"Something, I think?" the Ghost insisted.

"No," said Scrooge—"no. I should like to be

able to say a word or two to my clerk just now. That's all."

His former self turned down the lamps as he gave utterance to the wish; and Scrooge and the Ghost again stood side by side in the open air.

"My time grows short," observed the Spirit. "Quick!"

This was not addressed to Scrooge, or to anyone whom he could see, but it produced an immediate effect. For again Scrooge saw himself. He was older now, a man in the prime of life. His face had not the harsh and rigid lines of later years, but it had begun to wear the signs of care and avarice. There was an eager, greedy, restless motion in the eye, which showed the passion that had taken root, and where the shadow of the growing tree would fall.

He was not alone, but sat by the side of a fair young girl in a mourning-dress, in whose eyes there were tears, which sparkled in the light that shone out of the Ghost of Christmas Past.

"It matters little," she said softly. "To you, very little. Another idol has displaced me; and if it can cheer and comfort you in time to come, as I would have tried to do, I have no just cause to grieve."

"What idol had displaced you?" he rejoined.

"A golden one."

"This is the even-handed dealing of the world!" he said. "There is nothing on which it is so hard as poverty; and there is nothing it professes to condemn with such severity as the pursuit of wealth!"

"You fear the world too much," she answered gently. "All your other hopes have merged into the hope of being beyond the chance of its sordid reproach. I have seen your nobler aspirations fall off one by one, until the master passion, Gain, engrosses you. Have I not?"

"What then?" he retorted. "Even if I have grown so much wiser, what then? I am not changed toward you."

She shook her head.

"Am I?"

"Our contract is an old one. It was made when we were both poor, and content to be so, until, in good season, we could improve our worldly fortune by our patient industry. You *are* changed. When it was made, you were another man."

"I was a boy," he said impatiently.

"Your own feeling tells you that you were not what you are," she returned. "I am. That which promised happiness when we were one in heart is fraught with misery now that we are two. How often and how keenly I have thought of this, I will not say. It is enough that I *have* thought of it, and can release you."

"Have I ever sought release?"

"In words? No. Never."

"In what, then?"

"In a changed nature, in an altered spirit, in

another atmosphere of life, another Hope as its great end. In everything that made my love of any worth or value in your sight. If this had never been between us," said the girl, looking mildly, but with steadiness, upon him, "tell me, would you seek me out and try to win me now? Ah, no!"

He seemed to yield to the justice of this supposition, in spite of himself. But he said, with a struggle, "You think not."

"I would gladly think otherwise if I could," she answered. "Heaven knows! When *I* have learned a Truth like this, I know how strong and irresistible it must be. But if you were free today, tomorrow, yesterday, can even I believe that you would choose a dowerless girl—you who, in your very confidence with her, weigh everything by Gain; or, choosing her, if for a moment you were false enough to your own guiding principle to do so, do I not know that your repentance and regret would surely follow? I do, and I release you. With a full heart, for the love of him you once were."

He was about to speak, but, with her head turned from him, she resumed:

"You may—the memory of what is past half makes me hope you will—have pain in this. A very, very brief time, and you will dismiss the recollection of it, gladly, as an unprofitable dream, from which it happened well that you awoke. May you be happy in the life you have chosen!"

She left him, and they parted.

"Spirit!" said Scrooge, "show me no more! Conduct me home. Why do you delight to torture me?"

"One shadow more!" exclaimed the Ghost.

"No more!" cried Scrooge—"no more. I don't wish to see it. Show me no more!"

But the relentless Ghost pinioned him in both his arms, and forced him to observe what happened next.

They were in another scene and place, a room, not very large or handsome, but full of comfort. Near to the winter fire sat a beautiful young girl, so like that last that Scrooge believed it was the same, until he saw *her*, now a comely matron, sitting opposite her daughter. The noise in this room was perfectly tumultuous, for there were more children there than Scrooge in his agitated state of mind could count; and, unlike the celebrated herd in the poem, they were not forty children conducting themselves like one, but every child was conducting itself like forty. The consequences were uproarious beyond belief; but no one seemed to care; on the contrary, the mother and daughter laughed heartily, and enjoyed it very much; and the latter, soon beginning to mingle in the sports, got pillaged by the young brigands most ruthlessly. What would I not have given to be one of them! Though I never could have been so rude, no, no! I wouldn't for the wealth of all the world have crushed that braided hair, and torn it down; and for the precious little shoe, I wouldn't have plucked it off, God bless my soul! to save my life. As to measuring her waist in sport, as they did, bold young brood, I couldn't have done it; I should have expected my arm to have grown round it for a punishment, and never come straight again. And yet I should have dearly liked, I own, to have touched her lips, to have questioned her, that she might have opened them, to have looked upon the lashes of her downcast eyes, and never raised a blush, to have let loose waves of hair, an inch of which would be a keepsake beyond price; in short, I should have liked, I do confess, to have had the lightest license of a child, and yet to have been man enough to know its value.

But now a knocking at the door was heard, and such a rush immediately ensued that she, with laughing face and plundered dress, was borne toward it, in the center of a flushed and boisterous group, just in time to greet the father, who came home attended by a man laden with Christmas toys and presents. Then the shouting and the struggling, and the onslaught that was made on the defenseless porter! The scaling him, with chairs for ladders, to dive into his pockets, despoil him of brown paper parcels, hold on tight by his cravat, hug him round the neck, pommel his back, and kick his legs in irrepressible affection! The shouts of wonder and delight with which the development of every package was received! The terrible announcement that the baby had been taken in the act of putting a doll's frying pan into his mouth, and was more than suspected of having swallowed a fictitious turkey, glued on a wooden platter! The immense relief of finding this a false alarm! The joy, and gratitude, and ecstasy! They are all indescribable alike. It is enough that, by degrees, the children and their emotions got out of the parlor, and, by one stair at a time, up to the top of the house, where they went to bed, and so subsided.

And now Scrooge looked on more attentively than ever, when the master of the house, having his daughter leaning fondly on him, sat down with her mother at his own fireside; and when he thought that such another creature, quite as graceful and as full of promise, might have called him father, and been a springtime in the haggard winter of his life, his sight grew very dim indeed.

"Belle," said the husband, turning to his wife with a smile. "I saw an old friend of yours this afternoon."

"Who was it?"

"Guess!"

"How can I? Tut, don't I know?" she added in the same breath, laughing as he laughed. "Mr. Scrooge."

"Mr. Scrooge it was. I passed his office window; and as it was not shut up, and he had a candle inside, I could scarcely help seeing him. His partner lies upon the point of death, I hear, and there he sat alone. Quite alone in the world, I do believe."

"Spirit!" said Scrooge, in a broken voice, "remove me from this place."

"I told you these were shadows of the things that have been," said the Ghost. "That they are what they are, do not blame me!"

"Remove me!" Scrooge exclaimed. "I cannot bear it!"

He turned upon the Ghost, and, seeing that it looked upon him with a face in which, in some strange way, there were fragments of all the faces it had shown him, wrestled with it.

"Leave me! Take me back! Haunt me no longer!"

In the struggle, if that can be called a struggle in which the Ghost, with no visible resistance on its own part, was undisturbed by any effort of its adversary, Scrooge observed that its light was burning high and bright, and dimly connecting that with its influence over him, he seized the extinguisher-cap, and by a sudden action pressed it down upon its head.

The spirit dropped beneath it, so that the extinguisher covered its whole form, but though

Scrooge pressed it down with all his force, he could not hide the light, which streamed from under it in an unbroken flood upon the ground.

He was conscious of being exhausted, and overcome by an .irresistible drowsiness, and further, of being in his own bedroom. He gave the cap a parting squeeze, in which his hand relaxed, and had barely time to reel to bed before he sank into a heavy sleep.

Stave Three
The Second of the Three Spirits

Awakening in the middle of a prodigiously tough snore, and sitting up in bed to get his thoughts together, Scrooge had no occasion to be told that the bell was again upon the stroke of One. He felt that he was restored to consciousness in the right nick of time, for the especial purpose of holding a conference with the second messenger dispatched to him through Marley's intervention. But, finding that he turned uncomfortably cold when he began to wonder which of his curtains this new specter would draw back, he put them every one aside with his own hands, and, lying down again, established a sharp lookout all round the bed. For he wished to challenge the Spirit on the moment of its appearance, and did not wish to be taken by surprise, and made nervous.

Gentlemen of the free-and-easy sort, who plume themselves on being acquainted with a move or two, and being usually equal to the time of day, express the wide range of their capacity for adventure by observing that they are good for anything from pitch-and-toss to manslaughter; between which opposite extremes, no doubt, there lies a tolerably wide and comprehensive range of subjects. Without venturing for Scrooge quite as hardily as this, I don't mind calling on you to believe that he was ready for a good broad field of strange appearances, and that nothing between a baby and a rhinoceros would have astonished him very much.

Now, being prepared for almost anything, he was not by any means prepared for nothing; and, consequently, when the bell struck One, and no shape appeared, he was taken with a violent fit of trembling. Five minutes, ten minutes, a quarter of an hour went by, yet nothing came. All this time he lay upon a bed, the very core and center of a blaze of ruddy light, which streamed upon it when the clock proclaimed the hour; and which, being only light, was more alarming than a dozen ghosts, as he was powerless to make out what it meant, or would be at and was sometimes apprehensive that he might be at that very moment an interesting case of spontaneous combustion, without having the consolation of knowing it. At last, however, he began to think—

as you or I would have thought at first; for it is always the person not in the predicament who knows what ought to have been done in it, and would unquestionably have done it too—at last, I say, he began to think that the source and secret of this ghostly light might be in the adjoining room, from whence, on further tracing it, it seemed to shine. This idea taking full possession of his mind, he got up softly, and shuffled in his slippers to the door.

The moment Scrooge's hand was on the lock, a strange voice called him by his name, and bade him enter. He obeyed.

It was his own room. There was no doubt about that. But it had undergone a surprising transformation. The walls and ceiling were so hung with living green that it looked a perfect grove; from every part of which bright, gleaming berries glistened. The crisp leaves of holly, mistletoe, and ivy reflected back the light, as if so many little mirrors had been scattered there, and such a mighty blaze went roaring up the chimney, as that dull petrifaction of a hearth had never known in Scrooge's time, or Marley's for many a winter season gone. Heaped up on the floor, to form a kind of throne, were turkeys, geese, game, poultry, brawn, great joints of meat, suckling-pigs, long wreaths of sausages, mince-pies, plum puddings, barrels of oysters, red-hot chestnuts, cherry-cheeked apples, juicy oranges, luscious pears, immense twelfth-cakes, and seething bowls of punch, that made the chamber dim with their delicious steam. In easy state upon this couch, there sat a jolly Giant, glorious to see who bore a glowing torch, in shape not unlike Plenty's horn, and held it up, high up, to shed its light on Scrooge, as he came peeping round the door.

"Come in!" exclaimed the Ghost—"come in! and know me better, man!"

Scrooge entered timidly, and hung his head before this Spirit. He was not the dogged Scrooge he had been and though the Spirit's eyes were clear and kind, he did not like to meet them.

"I am the Ghost of Christmas Present," said the Spirit. "Look upon me!"

Scrooge reverently did so. It was clothed in one simple, deep-green robe, or mantle, bordered with white fur. This garment hung so loosely on the figure that its capacious breast was bare, as if disdaining to be warded or concealed by any artifice. Its feet, observable beneath the ample folds of the garment, were also bare, and on its head it wore no other covering than a holly wreath, set here and there with shining icicles. Its dark-brown curls were long and free, free as its genial face, its sparkling eyes, its open hand, its cheery voice, its unconstrained demeanor, and its joyful air. Girded round its middle was an antique scabbard, but no sword was in it, and the ancient sheath was eaten up with rust.

"You have never seen the like of me before!" exclaimed the Spirit.

"Never," Scrooge made answer to it.

"Have never walked forth with the younger members of my family, meaning (for I am very young) my elder brothers born in these later years?" pursued the Phantom.

"I don't think I have," said Scrooge. "I am afraid I have not. Have you had many brothers, Spirit?"

"More than eighteen hundred," said the Ghost.

"A tremendous family to provide for," muttered Scrooge.

The Ghost of Christmas Present rose.

"Spirit," said Scrooge submissively, "conduct me where you will. I went forth last night on compulsion, and I learned a lesson which is working now. Tonight, if you have aught to teach me, let me profit by it."

"Touch my robe!"

Scrooge did as he was told, and held it fast.

Holly, mistletoe, red berries, ivy, turkeys, geese, game, poultry, brawn, meat, pigs, sausages, oysters, pies, puddings, fruit, and punch, all vanished instantly. So did the room, the fire, the ruddy glow, the hour of the night, and they stood in the city streets on Christmas morning, where (for the weather was severe) the people made a rough, but brisk and not unpleasant kind of music, in scraping the snow from the pavement in front of their dwellings, and from the tops of their houses, when it was mad delight to the boys to see it come plumping down into the road below, and splitting into artificial little snowstorms.

The house-fronts looked black enough, and the windows blacker, contrasting with the smooth white sheet of snow upon the roofs, and with the dirtier snow upon the ground which last deposit had been plowed up in deep furrows by the heavy wheels of carts and wagons, furrows that crossed and recrossed each other hundreds of times where the great streets branched off, and made intricate channels, hard to trace, in the thick yellow mud and icy water. The sky was gloomy, and the shortest streets were choked up with a dingy mist, half thawed, half frozen, whose heavier particles descended in a shower of sooty atoms, as if all the chimneys in Great Britain had, by one consent, caught fire, and were blazing away to their dear hearts' content. There was nothing very cheerful in the climate or the town, and yet there was an air of cheerfulness abroad that the clearest summer air and brightest summer sun might have endeavored to diffuse in vain.

For the people who were shoveling away on the housetops were jovial and full of glee, calling out to one another from the parapets, and now and then exchanging a facetious snowball—better-natured missile far than many a wordy jest—

laughing heartily if it went right, and not less heartily if it went wrong. The poulterers' shops were still half open, and the fruiterers' were radiant in their glory. There were great, round, pot-bellied baskets of chestnuts, shaped like the waistcoats of jolly old gentlemen, lolling at the doors, and tumbling out into the street in their apoplectic opulence. There were ruddy, brown-faced broad-girthed Spanish onions, shining in the fatness of their growth like Spanish friars, and winking from their shelves in wanton slyness at the girls as they went by, and glanced demurely at the hung-up mistletoe. There were pears and apples, clustered high in blooming pyramids; there were bunches of grapes, made, in the shopkeepers' benevolence, to dangle from conspicuous hooks, that people's mouths might water gratis as they passed; there were piles of filberts, mossy and brown, recalling, in their fragrance, ancient walks among the woods, and pleasant shufflings ankle-deep through withered leaves; there were Norfolk biffins, squab and swarthy, setting off the yellow of the oranges and lemons, and, the great compactness of their juicy persons, urgently entreating and beseeching to be carried home in paper bags and eaten after dinner. The very gold and silverfish, set forth among these choice fruits in a bowl, though members of a dull and stagnant-blooded race, appeared to know that there was something going on and, to a fish, went gasping round and round their little world in slow and passionless excitement.

The grocers! oh, the grocers! nearly closed, with perhaps two shutters down, or one, but through these gaps such glimpses! It was not alone that the scales descending on the counter made a merry sound, or that the twine and roller parted company so briskly, or that the canisters were rattled up and down like juggling tricks, or even that the blended scents of tea and coffee were so grateful to the nose, or even that the raisins were so plentiful and rare, the almonds so extremely white, the sticks of cinnamon so long and straight, the other spices so delicious, the candied fruits so caked and spotted with molten sugar as to make the coldest lookers-on feel faint, and subsequently bilious. Nor was it that the figs were moist and pulpy, or that the French plums blushed in modest tartness from their highly decorated boxes, or that everything was good to eat and in its Christmas dress, but the customers were all so hurried and so eager in the hopeful promise of the day, that they tumbled up against each other at the door, crashing their wicker baskets wildly, and left their purchases upon the counter, and came running back to fetch them, and committed hundreds of the like mistakes, in the best humor possible; while the grocer and his people were so frank and fresh that the polished hearts with which they fastened their aprons behind might have been their own, worn outside for general inspection, and for Christmas daws to peck at, if they chose.

But soon the steeples called good people all to church and chapel, and away they came, flocking through the street in their best clothes, and with their gayest faces. And at the same time there emerged from scores of by-streets, lanes, and nameless turnings, innumerable people, carrying their dinners to the bakers' shops. The sight of these poor revelers appeared to interest the Spirit very much, for he stood, with Scrooge beside him, in the baker's doorway, and taking off the covers as their bearers passed, sprinkled incense on their dinners from his torch. And it was a very uncommon kind of torch, for once or twice when there were angry words between some dinner-carriers who had jostled each other, he shed a few drops of water on them from it, and their good humor was restored directly. For they said, it was a shame to quarrel upon Christmas Day. And so it was! God love it, so it was!

In time the bells ceased, and the bakers were shut up, and yet there was a genial shadowing forth of all these dinners, and the progress of their cooking, in the thawed blotch of wet above each baker's oven, where the pavement smoked as if its stones were cooking too.

"Is there a peculiar flavor in what you sprinkle from your torch?" asked Scrooge.

"There is. My own."

"Would it apply to any kind of dinner on this day?" asked Scrooge.

"To any kindly given. To a poor one most."

"Why to a poor one most?" asked Scrooge.

"Because it needs it most."

"Spirit," said Scrooge, after a moment's thought, "I wonder you, of all the beings in the many worlds about us, should desire to cramp these people's opportunities of innocent enjoyment."

"I!" cried the Spirit.

"You would deprive them of their means of dining every seventh day, often the only day on which they can be said to dine at all," said Scrooge, "wouldn't you?"

"I!" cried the Spirit.

"You seek to close these places on the Seventh Day," said Scrooge. "And it comes to the same thing."

"*I* seek!" exclaimed the Spirit.

"Forgive me if I am wrong. It has been done in your name, or at least in that of your family," said Scrooge.

"There are some upon this earth of yours," returned the Spirit, "who claim to know us, and who do their deeds of passion, pride, ill will, hatred, envy, bigotry, and selfishness in our name, who are as strange to us, and all our kith and kin, as if they had never lived. Remember that, and charge their doings on themselves, not us."

Scrooge promised that he would and they went on, invisible, as they had been before, into the suburbs of the town. It was a remarkable quality of the Ghost (which Scrooge had observed at the baker's), that notwithstanding his gigantic size, he could accommodate himself to any place with ease, and that he stood beneath a low roof quite as gracefully, and like a supernatural creature, as it was possible he could have done in any lofty hall.

And perhaps it was the pleasure the good Spirit had in showing off this power of his, or else it was his own kind, generous, hearty nature, and his sympathy with all poor men, that led him straight to Scrooge's clerk's; for there he went, and took Scrooge with him, holding to his robe and on the threshold of the door the Spirit smiled, and stopped to bless Bob Cratchit's dwelling with the sprinklings of his torch. Think of that! Bob had but fifteen "Bob" a week himself; he pocketed on Saturdays but fifteen copies of his Christian name and yet the Ghost of Christmas Present blessed his four-roomed house!

Then up rose Mrs. Cratchit, Cratchit's wife, dressed out but poorly in a twice-turned gown, but brave in ribbons, which are cheap and make a goodly show for sixpence, and she laid the cloth, assisted by Belinda Cratchit, second of her daughters, also brave in ribbons, while Master Peter Cratchit plunged a fork into the saucepan of potatoes, and getting the corners of his monstrous shirt-collar (Bob's private property, conferred upon his son and heir in honor of the day) into his mouth, rejoiced to find himself so gallantly attired, and yearned to show his linen in the fashionable Parks. And now two smaller Cratchits, boy and girl, came tearing in, screaming that outside the baker's they had smelled the goose, and known it for their own and, basking in luxurious thoughts of sage and onion, these young Cratchits danced about the table and exalted Master Peter Cratchit to the skies, while he (not proud, although his collars nearly choked him) blew the fire, until the slow potatoes, bubbling up, knocked loudly at the saucepan lid to be let out and peeled.

"What has ever got your precious father, then?" said Mrs. Cratchit. "And your brother, Tiny Tim? And Martha warn't as late last Christmas Day by half an hour!"

"Here's Martha, mother," said a girl, appearing as she spoke.

"Here's Martha, mother!" cried the two young Cratchits. "Hurrah! There's *such* goose, Martha!"

"Why, bless your heart alive, my dear, how late you are!" said Mrs. Cratchit, kissing her a dozen times, and taking off her shawl and bonnet for her with officious zeal.

"We'd a deal of work to finish up last night," replied the girl, "and had to clear away this morning, mother!"

"Well! Never mind so long as you are come," said Mrs. Cratchit. "Sit ye down before the fire, my dear, and have a warm, Lord bless ye!"

"No, no! There's father coming," cried the two young Cratchits, who were everywhere at once. "Hide, Martha, hide!"

So Martha hid herself, and in came little Bob, the father, with at least three feet of comforter, exclusive of the fringe, hanging down before him, and his threadbare clothes darned up and brushed, to look seasonable, and Tiny Tim upon his shoulder. Alas for Tiny Tim, he bore a little crutch, and had his limbs supported by an iron frame!

"Why, where's our Martha?" cried Bob Cratchit, looking round.

"Not coming," said Mrs. Cratchit.

"Not coming!" said Bob, with a sudden declension in his high spirits for he had been Tim's blood-horse all the way from church, and had come home rampant. "Not coming upon Christmas Day!"

Martha didn't like to see him disappointed, if it were only a joke; so she came out prematurely behind the closet door, and ran into his arms, while the two young Cratchits hustled Tiny Tim, and bore him off into the washhouse, that he might hear the pudding singing in the copper.

"And how did little Tim behave?" asked Mrs. Cratchit, when she had rallied Bob on his credulity, and Bob had hugged his daughter to his heart's content.

"As good as gold," said Bob, "and better. Somehow he gets thoughtful, sitting by himself so much, and thinks the strangest things you ever heard. He told me, coming home, that he hoped the people saw him in the church, because he was a cripple, and it might be pleasant to them to remember, upon Christmas Day, who made lame beggars walk and blind men see."

Bob's voice was tremulous when he told them this, and trembled more when he said that Tiny Tim was growing strong and hearty.

His active little crutch was heard upon the floor, and back came Tiny Tim before another word was spoken, escorted by his brother and sister to his stool beside the fire, and while Bob, turning up his cuffs—as if, poor fellow, they were capable of being made more shabby—compounded some hot mixture in a jug with gin and lemons, and stirred it round and round, and put it on the hob to simmer. Master Peter and the two ubiquitous young Cratchits went to fetch the goose, with which they soon returned in high procession.

Such a bustle ensued that you might have thought a goose the rarest of all birds, a feathered phenomenon, to which a black swan was a matter of course—and in truth it was something very like it in that house. Mrs. Cratchit made the gravy (ready beforehand in a little saucepan) hissing hot, Master Peter mashed the potatoes with incredible vigor, Miss Belinda sweetened up the applesauce, Martha dusted the hot plates, Bob took Tiny Tim beside him in a tiny corner at the table, the two young Cratchits set chairs for everybody, not forgetting themselves, and, mounting guard upon their posts, crammed spoons into their mouths, lest they should shriek for goose before their turn came to be helped. At last the dishes were set on, and grace was said. It was succeeded by a breathless pause, as Mrs. Cratchit, looking all along the carving-knife, prepared to plunge it in the breast, but when she did, and when the long-expected gush of stuffing issued forth, one murmer of delight arose all round the board, and even Tiny Tim, excited by the two young Cratchits, beat on the table with the handle of his knife, and feebly cried Hurrah!

There never was such a goose. Bob said he didn't believe there ever was such a goose cooked. Its tenderness and flavor, size and cheapness, were the themes of universal admiration. Eked out by applesauce and mashed potatoes, it was a sufficient dinner for the whole family; indeed, as Mrs. Cratchit said with great delight (surveying one small atom of a bone upon the dish), they hadn't ate it all at last! Yet everyone had enough, and the youngest Cratchits in particular were steeped in sage and onion to the eyebrows! But now, the plates being changed by Miss Belinda, Mrs. Cratchit left the room alone—too nervous to bear witness—to take the pudding up, and bring it in.

Suppose it should not be done enough! Suppose it should break in turning out! Suppose somebody should have got over the wall of the backyard, and stolen it, while they were merry with the goose—a supposition at which the two young Cratchits became livid! All sorts of horrors were supposed.

Hallo! A great deal of steam! The pudding was out of the copper. A smell like a washing-day! That was the cloth. A smell like an eating-house and a pastry-cook's next door to each other, with a laundress's next door to that! That was the pudding! In half a minute Mrs. Cratchit entered— flushed, but smiling proudly—with the pudding, like a speckled cannonball, so hard and firm, blazing in half of half-a-quartern of ignited brandy, and bedight with Christmas holly stuck into the top.

Oh, a wonderful pudding! Bob Cratchit said, and calmly, too, that he regarded it as the greatest success achieved by Mrs. Cratchit since their marriage. Mrs. Cratchit said that, now the weight was off her mind, she would confess she had her doubts about the quantity of flour. Everybody had something to say about it, but nobody said or thought it was at all a small pudding for a large family. It would have been flat heresy to do so. Any Cratchit would have blushed to hint at such a thing.

At last the dinner was all done, the cloth was cleared, the hearth swept, and the fire made up. The compound in the jug being tasted, and considered perfect, apples and oranges were put upon the table, and a shovelful of chestnuts on the fire. Then all the Cratchit family drew round the hearth in what Bob Cratchit called a circle, meaning half a one, and at Bob Cratchit's elbow stood the family display of glass—two tumblers and a custard-cup without a handle.

These held the hot stuff from the jug, however, as well as golden goblets would have done and Bob served it out with beaming looks, while the chestnuts on the fire sputtered and crackled noisily. Then Bob proposed:

"A merry Christmas to us all, my dears. God bless us!"

Which all the family re-echoed.

"God bless us, every one!" said Tiny Tim, the last of all.

He sat very close to his father's side, upon his little stool. Bob held his withered little hand in his, as if he loved the child, and wished to keep him by his side, and dreaded that he might be taken from him.

"Spirit," said Scrooge, with an interest he had

never felt before, "tell me if Tiny Tim will live."

"I see a vacant seat," replied the Ghost, "in the poor chimney-corner, and a crutch without an owner, carefully preserved. If these shadows remain unaltered by the Future, the child will die."

"No, no," said Scrooge. "Oh, no, kind Spirit! say he will be spared."

"If these shadows remain unaltered by the Future, none other of my race," returned the Ghost, "will find him here. What then? If he be like to die, he had better do it, and decrease the population."

Scrooge hung his head to hear his own words quoted by the Spirit, and was overcome with penitence and grief.

"Man," said the Ghost, "if man you be in heart, not adamant, forebear that wicked cant until you have discovered what the surplus is, and where it is. Will you decide what men shall live, what men shall die? It may be that in the sight of Heaven you are more worthless and less fit to live than millions like this poor man's child. O God! to hear the insect on the leaf pronouncing on the too much life among his hungry brothers in the dust!"

Scrooge bent before the Ghost's rebuke, and, trembling, cast his eyes upon the ground. But he raised them speedily, on hearing his own name.

"Mr. Scrooge!" said Bob; "I'll give you Mr. Scrooge, the Founder of the Feast!"

"The Founder of the Feast, indeed!" cried Mrs. Cratchit, reddening. "I wish I had him here. I'd give him a piece of my mind to feast upon, and I hope he'd have a good appetite for it."

"My dear," said Bob, "the children! Christmas Day."

"It should be Christmas Day, I am sure," said she, "on which one drinks the health of such an odious, stingy, hard, unfeeling man as Mr. Scrooge. You know he is, Robert! Nobody knows it better than you do, poor fellow!"

"My dear," was Bob's mild answer, "Christmas Day."

"I'll drink to his health for your sake, and the Day's," said Mrs. Cratchit, "not for his. Long life to him! A merry Christmas and a happy New Year! He'll be very merry and very happy, I have no doubt!"

The children drank the toast after her. It was the first of their proceedings which had no heartiness in it. Tiny Tim drank it last of all, but he didn't care twopence for it. Scrooge was the Ogre of the family. The mention of his name cast a dark shadow on the party, which was not dispelled for full five minutes.

After it had passed away, they were ten times merrier than before, from the mere relief of Scrooge the Baleful being done with. Bob Cratchit told them how he had a situation in his eye for Master Peter, which would bring in, if obtained, full five and sixpence weekly. The two young Cratchits laughed tremendously at the idea of Peter's being a man of business, and Peter himself looked thoughtfully at the fire from between his collars, as if he were deliberating what particular investments he should favor when he came into the receipt of that bewildering income. Martha, who was a poor apprentice at a milliner's, then told them what kind of work she had to do, and how many hours she worked at a stretch, and how she meant to lie abed tomorrow morning for a good long rest, tomorrow being a holiday she passed at home. Also how she had seen a countess and a lord some days before, and how the lord "was much about as tall as Peter"; at which Peter pulled up his collars so high that you couldn't have seen his head if you had been there. All this time the chestnuts and the jug went round and round, and by and by they had a song, about a lost child traveling in the snow, from Tiny Tim, who had a plaintive little voice, and sang it very well indeed.

There was nothing of high mark in this. They were not a handsome family, they were not well dressed, their shoes were far from being waterproof, their clothes were scanty, and Peter might have known, and very likely did, the inside of a pawnbroker's. But they were happy, grateful, pleased with one another, and contented with the time; and when they faded, and looked happier yet in the bright sprinklings of the Spirit's torch at parting, Scrooge had his eye upon them, and especially on Tiny Tim, until the last.

By this time it was getting dark and snowing pretty heavily, and as Scrooge and the Spirit went along the streets, the brightness of the roaring fires in kitchens, parlors, and all sorts of rooms was wonderful. Here, the flickering of the blaze showed preparations for a cozy dinner, with hot plates baking through and through before the fire, and deep-red curtains, ready to be drawn to shut out cold and darkness. There, all the children of the house were running out into the snow to meet their married sisters, brothers, cousins, uncles, aunts, and be the first to greet them. Here, again, were shadows on the window blinds of guests assembling and there a group of handsome girls, all hooded and fur-booted, and all chattering at once, tripped lightly off to some near neighbor's house, where, woe upon the single man who saw them enter—artful witches! well they knew it—in a glow.

But, if you had judged from the numbers of people on their way to friendly gatherings, you might have thought that no one was at home to give them welcome when they got there, instead of every house expecting company, and piling up its fires half-chimney high. Blessings on it, how the Ghost exulted! How it bared its breadth of breast, and opened its capacious palm, and floated on, outpouring, with a generous hand, its bright and harmless mirth on everything within its reach! The very lamplighter, who ran on before, dotting the dusky street with specks of light, and who was dressed to spend the evening somewhere, laughed out loudly as the Spirit passed, though little kenned the lamplighter that he had any company but Christmas!

And now, without a word of warning from the Ghost, they stood upon a bleak and desert moor, where monstrous masses of rude stone were cast about, as though it were the burial-place of giants, and water spread itself wheresoever it listed, or would have done so, but for the frost that held it prisoner, and nothing grew but moss and furze, and coarse, rank grass. Down in the west the setting sun had left a streak of fiery red, which glared upon the desolation for an instant, like a sullen eye, and, frowning lower, lower, lower yet, was lost in the thick gloom of darkest night.

"What place is this?" said Scrooge.

"A place where miners live, who labor in the bowels of the earth," returned the Spirit. "But they know me. See!"

A light shone from the window of a hut, and swiftly they advanced toward it. Passing through the wall of mud and stone, they found a cheerful company assembled round a glowing fire. An old, old man and woman with their children and their children's children, and another generation beyond that, all decked out gaily in their holiday attire. The old man, in a voice that seldom rose above the howling of the wind upon the barren waste, was singing them a Christmas song—it had been a very old song when he was a boy—and from time to time they all joined in the chorus. So surely as they raised their voices, the old man got quite blithe and loud, and so surely as they stopped, his vigor sank again.

The Spirit did not tarry here, but bade Scrooge hold his robe, and, passing on above the moor, sped—whither? Not to sea? To sea. To Scrooge's horror, looking back, he saw the last of the land, a frightful range of rocks, behind them and his ears were deafened by the thundering of water, as it rolled, and roared, and raged among the dreadful caverns it had worn, and fiercely tried to undermine the earth.

Built upon a dismal reef of sunken rocks, some leagues or so from shore, on which the waters chafed and dashed, the wild year through, there stood a solitary lighthouse. Great heaps of seaweed clung to its base, and storm-birds—born of the wind, one might suppose, as seaweed of the water—rose and fell about it, like the waves they skimmed.

But even here, two men who watched the light had made a fire, that through the loophole in the thick stone wall shed out a ray of brightness on the awful sea. Joining their horny hands over the rough table at which they sat, they wished each other Merry Christmas in their can of grog, and one of them, the elder, too, with his face all damaged and scarred with hard weather, as the figure-head of an old ship might be, struck up a sturdy song that was like a gale in itself.

Again the Ghost sped on, above the black and heaving sea—on, on—until, being far away, as he told Scrooge, from any shore, they lighted on a ship. They stood beside the helmsman at the wheel, the lookout in the bow, the officers who had the watch, dark, ghostly figures in their several stations, but every man among them hummed a Christmas tune, or had a Christmas thought, or spoke below his breath to his companion of some bygone Christmas Day, with homeward hopes belonging to it. And every man on board, waking or sleeping, good or bad, had had a kinder word for one another on that day in the year, and had shared to some extent in its festivities, and had remembered those he cared for at a distance, and had known that they delighted to remember him.

It was a great surprise to Scrooge, while listening to the moaning of the wind, and thinking what a solemn thing it was to move on through the lonely darkness over an unknown abyss, whose depths were secrets as profound as death—it was a great surprise to Scrooge, while thus engaged, to hear a hearty laugh. It was a much greater surprise to Scrooge to recognize it as his own nephew's and to find himself in a bright, dry, gleaming room, with the Spirit standing smiling by his side, and looking at that same nephew with approving affability!

"Ha, ha!" laughed Scrooge's nephew. "Ha, ha, ha!"

If you should happen, by any unlikely chance, to know a man more blessed in a laugh than Scrooge's nephew, all I can say is, I should like to know him, too. Introduce him to me, and I'll cultivate his acquaintance.

It is a fair, even-handed, noble adjustment of things, that, while there is infection in disease and sorrow, there is nothing in the world so irresistibly contagious as laughter and good humor. When Scrooge's nephew laughed in this way, holding his sides, rolling his head, and twisting his face into the most extravagant contortions. Scrooge's niece, by marriage, laughed as heartily as he. And their assembled friends, being not a bit behind-hand, roared out lustily.

"Ha, ha! Ha, ha, ha, ha!"

"He said that Christmas was a humbug, as I live!" cried Scrooge's nephew. "He believed it, too!"

"More shame for him, Fred!" said Scrooge's niece indignantly. Bless those women, they never do anything by halves. They are always in earnest.

She was very pretty; exceedingly pretty. With a

dimpled, surprised-looking capital face, a ripe little mouth that seemed made to be kissed—as no doubt it was, all kinds of good little dots about her chin, that melted into one another when she laughed, and the sunniest pair of eyes you ever saw in any little creature's head. Altogether she was what you would have called provoking, you know, but satisfactory, too. Oh, perfectly satisfactory!

"He's a comical old fellow," said Scrooge's nephew, "that's the truth; and not so pleasant as he might be. However, his offenses carry their own punishment, and I have nothing to say against him."

"I'm sure he is very rich, Fred," hinted Scrooge's niece. "At least you always tell *me* so."

"What of that, my dear?" said Scrooge's nephew. "His wealth is of no use to him. He doesn't do any good with it. He doesn't make himself comfortable with it. He hasn't the satisfaction of thinking—ha, ha, ha!—that he is ever going to benefit us with it."

"I have no patience with him," observed Scrooge's niece. Scrooge's niece's sisters, and all the other ladies, expressed the same opinion.

"Oh, I have!" said Scrooge's nephew. "I am sorry for him: I couldn't be angry with him if I tried. Who suffers by his ill whims? Himself, always. Here, he takes it into his head to dislike us, and he won't come and dine with us. What's the consequence? He doesn't lose much of a dinner."

"Indeed, I think he loses a very good dinner," interrupted Scrooge's niece. Everybody else said the same, and they must be allowed to have been competent judges, because they had just had dinner and, with the dessert upon the table, were clustered round the fire, by lamplight.

"Well! I am very glad to hear it," said Scrooge's nephew, "because I haven't any great faith in these young housekeepers. What do *you* say, Topper?"

Topper had clearly got his eye upon one of Scrooge's niece's sisters, for he answered that a bachelor was a wretched outcast, who had no right to express an opinion on the subject. Whereat Scrooge's niece's sister—the plump one with the lace tucker, not the one with the roses—blushed.

"Do go on, Fred," said Scrooge's niece, clapping her hands. "He never finishes what he begins to say! He is such a ridiculous fellow!"

Scrooge's nephew reveled in another laugh, and as it was impossible to keep the infection off, though the plump sister tried hard to do it with aromatic vinegar, his example was unanimously followed.

"I was only going to say," said Scrooge's nephew, "that the consequence of taking a dislike to us, and not making merry with us, is, as I think, that he loses some pleasant moments, which could do him no harm. I am sure he loses pleasanter companions than he can find in his own thoughts, either in his moldy old office or his dusty chambers. I mean to give him the same chance every year, whether he likes it or not, for I pity him. He may rail at Christmas till he dies, but he can't help thinking better of it—I defy him—if he finds me going there, in good temper, year after year, and saying, 'Uncle Scrooge, how are you?' If it only puts him in the vein to leave his poor clerk fifty pounds, *that's* something, and I think I shook him, yesterday.''

It was their turn to laugh now, at the notion of his shaking Scrooge. But being thoroughly good-natured, and not much caring what they laughed at, so that they laughed at any rate, he encouraged them in their merriment, and passed the bottle, joyously.

After tea, they had some music. For they were a musical family, and knew what they were about, when they sung a glee or catch, I can assure you: especially Topper, who could growl away in the bass like a good one, and never swell the large veins in his forehead, or get red in the face over it. Scrooge's niece played well upon the harp and played, among other tunes, a simple little air (a mere nothing; you might learn to whistle it in two minutes) which had been familiar to the child who fetched Scrooge from the boarding-school, as he had been reminded by the Ghost of Christmas

Past. When this strain of music sounded, all the things that Ghost had shown him came upon his mind; he softened more and more and thought that if he could have listened to it often, years ago, he might have cultivated the kindness of life for his own happiness with his own hands, without resorting to the sexton's spade that buried Jacob Marley.

But they didn't devote the whole evening to music. After a while they played at forfeits, for it is good to be children sometimes, and never better than at Christmas, when its mighty Founder was a child himself. Stop! There was first a game at blindman's-buff. Of course there was. And I no more believe Topper was really blind than I believe he had eyes in his boots. My opinion is, that it was a done thing between him and Scrooge's nephew, and that the Ghost of Christmas Present knew it. The way he went after that plump sister in the lace tucker was an outrage on the credulity of human nature. Knocking down the fire-irons, tumbling over the chairs, bumping up against the piano, smothering himself among the curtains, wherever she went, there went he! He always knew where the plump sister was. He wouldn't catch anybody else. If you had fallen up against him (as some of them did) on purpose, he would have made a feint of endeavoring to seize you, which would have been an affront to your understanding, and would instantly have sidled off in the direction of the plump sister. She often cried out that it wasn't fair, and it really was not. But when, at last, he caught her; when, in spite of all her silken rustlings, and her rapid flutterings past him, he got her into a corner whence there was no escape, then his conduct was the most execrable. For his pretending not to know her, his pretending that it was necessary to touch her headdress, and further to assure himself of her identity by pressing a certain ring upon her finger, and a certain chain about her neck, was vile, monstrous! No doubt she told him her opinion of it, when, another blind man being in office, they were so very confidential together, behind the curtains.

Scrooge's niece was not one of the blindman's-buff party, but was made comfortable with a large chair and a footstool, in a snug corner, where the Ghost and Scrooge were close behind her. But she joined in the forfeits, and loved her love to admiration with all the letters of the alphabet. Likewise at the game of How, When, and Where, she was very great, and, to the secret joy of Scrooge's nephew, beat her sisters hollow, though they were sharp girls, too, as Topper could have told you. There might have been twenty people there, young and old, but they all played, and so did Scrooge for, wholly forgetting, in the interest he had in what was going on, that his voice made no sound in their ears, he sometimes came out with his guess quite loud, and very often guessed right, too; for the sharpest needle, best White-chapel, warranted not to cut in the eye was not sharper than Scrooge, blunt as he took it in his head to be.

The Ghost was greatly pleased to find him in this mood, and looked upon him with such favor, that he begged like a boy to be allowed to stay until the guests departed. But this the spirit said could not be done.

"Here is a new game," said Scrooge. "One half hour, Spirit, only one!"

It was a game called Yes and No, where Scrooge's nephew had to think of something, and the rest must find out what, he only answering to their questions yes or no, as the case was. The brisk fire of questioning to which he was exposed, elicited from him that he was thinking of an animal, a live animal, rather a disagreeable animal, a savage animal, an animal that growled and grunted sometimes, and talked sometimes, and lived in London, and walked about the streets, and wasn't made a show of, and wasn't led by anybody, and didn't live in a menagerie, and was never killed in a market, and was not a horse, or an ass, or a cow, or a bull, or a tiger, or a dog, or a pig, or a cat, or a bear. At every fresh question that was put to him, this nephew burst into a fresh roar of laughter and was so inexpressibly tickled, that he was obliged to get up off the sofa and stamp. At last the plump sister, falling into a similar state, cried out:

"I have found it out! I know what it is, Fred! I know what it is!"

"What is it?" cried Fred.

"It's your Uncle Scro-o-o-oge!"

Which it certainly was. Admiration was the universal sentiment, though some objected that the reply to "Is it a bear?" ought to have been "Yes," inasmuch as the answer in the negative was sufficient to have diverted their thoughts from Mr. Scrooge, supposing they had ever had any tendency that way.

"He has given us plenty of merriment, I am sure," said Fred, "and it would be ungrateful not to drink his health. Here is a glass of mulled wine ready to our hand at the moment and I say, 'Uncle Scrooge!'"

"Well! Uncle Scrooge!" they cried.

"A Merry Christmas and a Happy New Year to the old man, whatever he is!" said Scrooge's nephew. "He wouldn't take it from me, but may he have it, nevertheless. Uncle Scrooge!"

Uncle Scrooge had imperceptibly become so gay and light of heart, that he would have pledged the unconscious company in return, and thanked them in an inaudible speech, if the Ghost had given him time. But the whole scene passed off in the breath of the last word spoken by his nephew, and he and the Spirit were again upon their travels.

Much they saw, and far they went, and many homes they visited, but always with a happy end. The Spirit stood beside sick-beds, and they were cheerful; on foreign lands, and they were close at home; by struggling men, and they were patient in their greater hope; by poverty, and it was rich. In almshouse, hospital, and jail, in misery's every refuge, where vain man in his little brief authority had not made fast the door, and barred the Spirit out, he left his blessing, and taught Scrooge his precepts.

It was a long night, if it were only a night, but Scrooge had his doubts of this, because the Christmas holidays appeared to be condensed into the space of time they passed together. It was strange, too, that while Scrooge remained unaltered in his outward form, the Ghost grew older, clearly older. Scrooge had observed this change, but never spoke of it, until they left a children's Twelfth Night party, when, looking at the Spirit as they stood together in an open place, he noticed that its hair was gray.

"Are spirits' lives so short?" said Scrooge.

"My life upon this globe is very brief," replied the Ghost. "It ends tonight."

89

"Tonight!" cried Scrooge.

"Tonight at midnight. Hark. The time is drawing near."

The chimes were ringing the three quarters past eleven at that moment.

"Forgive me if I am not justified in what I ask," said Scrooge, looking intently at the Spirit's robe "but I see something strange, and not belonging to yourself, protruding from your skirts. Is it a foot or a claw?"

"It might be a claw, for the flesh there is upon it," was the Spirit's sorrowful reply. "Look here."

From the foldings of its robe, it brought two children, wretched, abject, frightful, hideous, miserable. They knelt down at its feet, and clung upon the outside of its garment.

"Oh, Man! look here! Look, look, down here!" exclaimed the Ghost.

They were a boy and a girl. Yellow, meager, ragged, scowling, wolfish; but prostrate, too, in their humility. Where graceful youth should have filled their features out, and touched them with its freshest tints, a stale and shriveled hand, like that of age, had pinched and twisted them, and pulled them into shreds. Where angels might have sat enthroned, devils lurked, and glared out menacing. No change, no degradation, no perversion of humanity, in any grade, through all the mysteries of wonderful creation, has monsters half so horrible and dread.

90

Scrooge started back, appalled. Having them shown to him in this way, he tried to say they were fine children, but the words choked themselves, rather than be parties to a lie of such enormous magnitude.

"Spirit! are they yours?" Scrooge could say no more.

"They are Man's," said the Spirit, looking down upon them. "And they cling to me, appealing from their fathers. This boy is Ignorance. This girl is Want. Beware of them both, and all of their degree, but most of all beware this boy, for on his brow I see that written which is Doom, unless the writing be erased. Deny it!" cried the Spirit, stretching out its hand toward the city. "Slander those who tell it ye! Admit it for your factious purposes, and make it worse! And bide the end!"

"Have they no refuge or resource?" cried Scrooge.

"Are there no prisons?" said the Spirit, turning on him for the last time with his own words. "Are there no workhouses?"

The bell struck Twelve.

Scrooge looked about him for the Ghost, and saw it not. As the last stroke ceased to vibrate, he remembered the prediction of old Jacob Marley, and, lifting up his eyes, beheld a solemn phantom, draped and hooded, coming, like a mist along the ground, toward him.

Stave Four
The Last of the Spirits

The Phantom slowly, gravely, silently, approached. When it came near him, Scrooge bent down upon his knee, for in the very air through which this spirit moved it seemed to scatter gloom and mystery.

It was shrouded in a deep black garment, which concealed its head, its face, its form, and left nothing of it visible save one outstretched hand. But for this it would have been difficult to detach its figure from the night, and separate it from the darkness by which it was surrounded.

He felt that it was tall and stately when it came beside him, and that its mysterious presence filled him with a solemn dread. He knew no more, for the Spirit neither spoke nor moved.

"I am in the presence of the Ghost of Christmas Yet to Come?" said Scrooge.

The Spirit answered not, but pointed onward with its hand.

"You are about to show me shadows of the things that have not happened, but will happen in the time before us," Scrooge pursued. "Is that so, Spirit?"

The upper portion of the garment was contracted for an instant in its folds, as if the Spirit had inclined its head. That was the only answer he received.

Although well used to ghostly company by this time, Scrooge feared the silent shape so much that his legs trembled beneath him, and he found that he could hardly stand when he prepared to follow it. The Spirit paused a moment, as if observing his condition, and giving him time to recover.

But Scrooge was all the worse for this. It thrilled him with a vague uncertain horror, to know that, behind the dusky shroud, there were ghostly eyes intently fixed upon him, while he, though he stretched his own to the utmost, could see nothing but a spectral hand and one great heap of black.

"Ghost of the Future!" he exclaimed, "I fear you more than any specter I have seen. But as I know your purpose is to do me good, and as I hope to live to be another man from what I was, I am prepared to bear you company, and do it with a thankful heart. Will you not speak to me?"

It gave him no reply. The hand was pointed straight before them.

"Lead on!" said Scrooge—"lead on! The night is waning fast, and it is precious time to me, I know. Lead on, Spirit!"

The Phantom moved away as it had come toward him. Scrooge followed in the shadow of its dress, which bore him up, he thought, and carried him along.

They scarcely seemed to enter the City, for the City rather seemed to spring up about them, and encompass them of its own act. But there they were, in the heart of it, on 'Change, among the merchants, who hurried up and down, and chinked the money in their pockets, and conversed in groups, and looked at their watches, and trifled thoughtfully with their gold seals, and so forth, as Scrooge had seen them often.

The Spirit stopped beside one little knot of businessmen. Observing that the hand was pointed to them, Scrooge advanced to listen to their talk.

"No," said a great fat man with a monstrous chin, "I don't know much about it either way. I only know he's dead."

"When did he die?" inquired another.

"Last night, I believe."

"Why, what was the matter with him?" asked a third, taking a vast quantity of snuff out of a very large snuff box. "I thought he'd never die."

"God knows," said the first, with a yawn.

"What has he done with his money?" said a red-faced gentleman with a pendulous excrescence on the end of his nose, that shook like the gills of a turkey-cock.

"I haven't heard," said the man with the large chin, yawning again. "Left it to his company, perhaps. He hasn't left it to *me*. That's all I know."

This pleasantry was received with a general laugh.

"It's likely to be a very cheap funeral," said the same speaker, "for, upon my life, I don't know of anybody to go to it. Suppose we make up a party, and volunteer?"

"I don't mind going if a lunch is provided," observed the gentleman with the excrescence on his nose. "But I must be fed, if I make one."

Another laugh.

"Well, I am the most disinterested among you, after all," said the first speaker, "For I never wear black gloves, and I never eat lunch. But I'll offer to go, if anybody else will. When I come to think of it, I'm not at all sure that I wasn't his most particular friend, for we used to stop and speak whenever we met. By-by!"

Speakers and listeners strolled away, and mixed with other groups. Scrooge knew the men, and looked toward the Spirit for an explanation.

The Phantom glided on into a street. Its finger

pointed to two persons meeting. Scrooge listened again, thinking that the explanation might lie here.

He knew these men, also, perfectly. They were men of business, very wealthy, and of great importance. He had made a point always of standing well in their esteem—in a business point of view, that is, strictly in a business point of view.

"How are you?" said one.

"How are you?" returned the other.

"Well!" said the first. "Old Scratch has got his own at last, hey?"

"So I am told," returned the second. "Cold, isn't it?"

"Seasonable for Christmas-time. You are not a skater, I suppose?"

"No. No. Something else to think of. Good morning!"

Not another word. That was their meeting, their conversation, and their parting.

Scrooge was at first inclined to be surprised that the Spirit should attach importance to conversations apparently so trivial, but feeling assured that they must have some hidden purpose, he set himself to consider what it was likely to be. They could scarcely be supposed to have any bearing on the death of Jacob, his old partner, for that was Past, and this Ghost's province was the Future. Nor could he think of anyone immediately connected with himself, to whom he could apply them. But nothing doubting that, to whomsoever they applied, they had some latent moral for his own improvement, he resolved to treasure up every word he heard, and everything he saw, and especially to observe the shadow of himself when it appeared. For he had an expectation that the conduct of his future self would give him the clue he missed, and would render the solution of these riddles easy.

He looked about in that very place for his own image, but another man stood in his accustomed corner, and though the clock pointed to his usual time of day for being there, he saw no likeness of himself among the multitudes that poured in through the Porch. It gave him little surprise, however, for he had been revolving in his mind a change of life, and thought and hoped he saw his newborn resolutions carried out in this.

Quiet and dark, beside him stood the Phantom, with its outstretched hand. When he roused himself from this thoughtful quest, he fancied, from the turn of the hand and its situation in reference to himself, that the Unseen Eyes were looking at him keenly. It made him shudder, and feel very cold.

They left the busy scene, and went into an obscure part of the town, where Scrooge had never penetrated before, although he recognized its situation, and its bad repute. The ways were foul and narrow, the shops and houses wretched, the people half naked, drunken, slipshod, ugly. Alleys and archways, like so many cesspools, disgorged their offenses of smell, and dirt, and life, upon the straggling streets; and the whole quarter reeked with crime, with filth and misery.

Far in this den of infamous resort, there was a low-browed, beetling shop, below a penthouse roof, where iron, old rags, bottles, bones, and greasy offal were bought. Upon the floor within were piled up heaps of rusty keys, nails, chains, hinges, files, scales, weights, and refuse iron of all kinds. Secrets that few would like to scrutinize were bred and hidden in mountains of unseemly rags, masses of corrupted fat, and sepulchers of bones. Sitting in among the wares he dealt in, by a charcoal stove, made of old bricks, was a gray-haired rascal, nearly seventy years of age, who had screened himself from the cold air without by a frowzy curtaining of miscellaneous tatters, hung upon a line, and smoked his pipe in all the luxury of calm retirement.

Scrooge and the Phantom came into the presence of this man, just as a woman with a heavy bundle slunk into the shop. But she had scarcely entered, when another woman, similarly laden, came in too, and she was closely followed by a man in faded black, who was no less startled by the sight of them than they had been upon the recognition of each other. After a short period of blank astonishment, in which the old man with the pipe had joined them, they all three burst into a laugh.

"Let the charwoman alone to be the first!" cried she who had entered first. "Let the laundress alone to be the second, and let the undertaker's man alone to be the third. Look here, old Joe, here's a chance! If we haven't all three met here without meaning it!"

"You couldn't have met in a better place," said old Joe, removing his pipe from his mouth. "Come into the parlor. You were made free of it long ago, you know, and the other two ain't strangers. Stop till I shut the door of the shop. Ah! How it shrieks! There ain't such a rusty bit of metal in the place as its own hinges, I believe, and I'm sure there's no such old bones here as mine. Ha, ha! We're all suitable to our calling, we're well matched. Come into the parlor. Come into the parlor."

The parlor was the space behind the screen of rags. The old man raked the fire together with an old stair-rod, and having trimmed his smoky lamp (for it was night) with the stem of his pipe, put it in his mouth again.

While he did this, the woman who had already spoken threw her bundle on the floor, and sat down in a flaunting manner on a stool, crossing her elbows on her knees, and looking with a bold defiance at the other two.

"What odds, then? What odds, Mrs. Dilber?"

said the woman. "Every person has a right to take care of themselves. *He* always did!"

"That's true, indeed!" said the laundress. "No man more so."

"Why, then, don't stand staring as if you was afraid, woman! Who's the wiser? We're not going to pick holes in each other's coats, I suppose?"

"No, indeed!" said Mrs. Dilber and the man together. "We should hope not."

"Very well, then!" cried the woman. "That's enough. Who's the worse for the loss of a few things like these? Not a dead man, I suppose?"

"No indeed," said Mrs. Dilber, laughing.

"If he wanted to keep 'em after he was dead, a wicked old screw," pursued the woman, "why wasn't he natural in his lifetime? If he had been, he'd have had somebody to look after him when he was struck with Death, instead of lying gasping out his last there, alone by himself."

"It's the truest word that ever was spoke," said Mrs. Dilber. "It's a judgment on him."

"I wish it was a little heavier judgment," replied the woman, "and it should have been, you may depend upon it, if I could have laid my hands on anything else. Open that bundle, old Joe, and let me know the value of it. Speak out plain. I'm not afraid to be the first, nor afraid for them to see it. We knew pretty well that we were helping ourselves before we met here, I believe. It's no sin. Open the bundle, Joe."

But the gallantry of her friends would not allow of this, and the man in faded black, mounting the breach first, produced *his* plunder. It was not extensive. A seal or two, a pencil-case, a pair of sleeve-buttons, and a brooch of no great value, were all. They were severally examined and appraised by old Joe, who chalked the sums he was disposed to give for each upon the wall, and added them up into a total when he found that there was nothing more to come.

"That's your account," said Joe, "and I wouldn't give another sixpence, if I was to be boiled for not doing it. Who's next?"

Mrs. Dilber was next. Sheets and towels, a little wearing-apparel, two old-fashioned silver teaspoons, a pair of sugar-tongs, and a few boots. Her account was stated on the wall in the same manner.

"I always give too much to ladies. It's a weakness of mine, and that's the way I ruin myself," said old Joe. "That's your account. If you asked me for another penny, and made it an open question, I'd repent of being so liberal, and knock off half a crown."

"And now undo *my* bundle, Joe," said the first woman.

Joe went down on his knees for the greater convenience of opening it, and, having unfastened a great many knots, dragged out a large, heavy roll of some dark stuff.

"What do you call this?" said Joe. "Bed-curtains?"

"Ah!" returned the woman, laughing and leaning forward on her crossed arms. "Bed-curtains!"

"You don't mean to say you took 'em down, rings and all, with him lying there?" said Joe.

"Yes, I do," replied the woman. "Why not?"

"You were born to make your fortune," said Joe, "and you'll certainly do it."

"I certainly sha'n't hold my hand, when I can get anything in it by reaching it out, for the sake of such a man as He was, I promise you, Joe," returned the woman coolly. "Don't drop that oil upon the blankets now."

"His blankets?" asked Joe.

"Whose else's do you think?" replied the woman. "He isn't likely to take cold without 'em, I dare say."

"I hope he didn't die of anything catching? Eh?" said old Joe, stopping in his work, and looking up.

"Don't be afraid of that," returned the woman. "I ain't so fond of his company that I'd loiter about him for such things, if he did. Ah! You may look through that shirt till your eyes ache; but you won't find a hole in it, nor a threadbare place. It's the best he had, and a fine one, too. They'd have wasted it, if it hadn't been for me."

"What do you call wasting of it?" asked old Joe.

"Putting it on him to be buried in, to be sure," replied the woman, with a laugh. "Somebody was fool enough to do it, but I took it off again. If calico ain't good enough for such a purpose, it isn't good enough for anything. It's quite as becoming to the body. He can't look uglier than he did in that one."

Scrooge listened to this dialogue in horror. As they sat grouped about their spoil, in the scanty light afforded by the old man's lamp, he viewed them with a detestation and disgust which could hardly have been greater though they had been obscene demons, marketing the corpse itself.

"Ha, ha!" laughed the same woman, when old Joe, producing a flannel bag with money in it, told out their several gains upon the ground. "This is the end of it, you see! He frightened everyone away from him when he was alive, to profit us when he was dead! Ha, ha, ha!"

"Spirit!" said Scrooge, shuddering from head to foot. "I see, I see. The case of this unhappy man might be my own. My life tends that way now. Merciful Heaven, what is this?"

He recoiled in terror, for the scene had changed, and now he almost touched a bed—a bare, uncurtained bed, on which, beneath a ragged sheet, there lay a something covered up, which, though it was dumb, announced itself in awful language.

The room was very dark, too dark to be observed

with any accuracy, though Scrooge glanced round it in obedience to a secret impulse, anxious to know what kind of room it was. A pale light, rising in the outer air, fell straight upon the bed, and on it, plundered and bereft, unwatched, unwept, uncared for, was the body of this man.

Scrooge glanced toward the Phantom. Its steady hand was pointed to the head. The cover was so carelessly adjusted that the slightest raising of it, the motion of a finger upon Scrooge's part, would have disclosed the face. He thought of it, felt how easy it would be to do, and longed to do it, but had no more power to withdraw the veil than to dismiss the specter at his side.

Oh cold, cold, rigid, dreadful Death, set up thine altar here, and dress it with such terrors as thou hast at thy command, for this thy dominion! But of the loved, revered, and honored head, thou canst not turn one hair to thy dread purposes, or make one feature odious. It is not that the hand is heavy, and will fall down when released; it is not that the heart and pulse are still: but that the hand was open, generous, and true, the heart brave, warm, and tender, and the pulse a man's. Strike, Shadow, strike! And see his good deeds springing from the wound, to sow the world with life immortal!

No voice pronounced these words in Scrooge's ears, and yet he heard them when he looked upon the bed. He thought, if this man could be raised up now, what would be his foremost thoughts? Avarice, hard dealing, griping cares? They have brought him to a rich end, truly!

He lay, in the dark, empty house, with not a man, a woman, or a child to say he was kind to me in this or that, and for the memory of one kind word I will be kind to him. A cat was tearing at the door, and there was a sound of gnawing rats beneath the hearthstone. What *they* wanted in the room of death, and why they were so restless and disturbed, Scrooge did not dare to think.

"Spirit!" he said, "this is a fearful place. In leaving it, I shall not leave its lesson, trust me. Let us go!"

Still the Ghost pointed with an unmoved finger to the head.

"I understand you," Scrooge returned, "and I would do it, if I could. But I have not the power, Spirit. I have not the power."

Again it seemed to look upon him.

"If there is any person in the town who feels emotion caused by this man's death," said Scrooge, quite agonized, "show that person to me, Spirit. I beseech you!"

The Phantom spread its dark robe before him for a moment, like a wing and withdrawing it, revealed a room by daylight, where a mother and her children were.

She was expecting someone, and with anxious eagerness: for she walked up and down the room, started at every sound, looked out from the window, glanced at the clock, tried, but in vain, to work with her needle, and could hardly bear the voices of her children in their play.

At length the long-expected knock was heard. She hurried to the door, and met her husband, a man whose face was care-worn and depressed, though he was young. There was a remarkable expression in it now, a kind of serious delight of which he felt ashamed, and which he struggled to repress.

He sat down to the dinner that she had been hoarding for him by the fire, and when she asked him faintly what news (which was not until after a long silence), he appeared embarrassed how to answer.

"Is it good," she said, "or bad?"—to help him.

"Bad," he answered.

"We are quite ruined?"

"No. There is hope yet, Caroline."

"If *he* relents," she said, amazed, "there is! Nothing is past hope, if such a miracle has happened."

"He is past relenting," said her husband. "He is dead."

She was a mild and patient creature, if her face spoke the truth; but she was thankful in her soul to hear it, and she said so, with clasped hands. She prayed forgiveness the next moment, and was sorry, but the first was the emotion of her heart.

"What the half-drunken woman whom I told you of last night said to me, when I tried to see him and obtain a week's delay, and what I thought was a mere excuse to avoid me, turns out to have been quite true. He was not only very ill, but dying, then."

"To whom will our debt be transferred?"

"I don't know. But before that time we shall be ready with the money and even though we were not, it would be bad fortune indeed to find so merciless a creditor in his successor. We may sleep tonight with light hearts, Caroline!"

Yes. Soften it as they would, their hearts were lighter. The children's faces, hushed and clustered round to hear what they so little understood, were brighter, and it was a happier house for this man's death! The only emotion that the Ghost could show him, caused by the event, was one of pleasure.

"Let me see some tenderness connected with a death," said Scrooge, "or that dark chamber, Spirit, which we left just now will be forever present to me."

The Ghost conducted him through several streets familiar to his feet and, as they went along, Scrooge looked here and there to find himself, but nowhere was he to be seen. They entered poor Bob Cratchit's house—the dwelling he had visited before—and found the mother and the children seated around the fire.

Quiet. Very quiet. The noisy little Cratchits were as still as statues in one corner, and sat looking up at Peter, who had a book before him. The mother and her daughters were engaged in sewing. But surely they were very quiet!

"'And he took a child, and set him in the midst of them.'"

Where had Scrooge heard those words? He had not dreamed them. The boy must have read them out, as he and the Spirit crossed the threshold. Why did he not go on?

The mother laid her work upon the table, and put her hand up to her face.

"The color hurts my eyes," she said.

The color? Ah, poor Tiny Tim!

"They're better now again," said Cratchit's wife. "It makes them weak by candlelight; and I wouldn't show weak eyes to your father when he comes home, for the world. It must be near his time."

"Past it, rather," Peter answered, shutting up his book. "But I think he has walked a little slower than he used, these few last evenings, mother."

They were very quiet again. At last she said, and in a steady, cheerful voice, that only faltered once:

"I have known him walk with—I have known him walk with Tiny Tim upon his shoulder very fast indeed."

"And so have I," cried Peter. "Often."

"And so have I," exclaimed another. So had all.

"But he was very light to carry," she resumed, intent upon her work, "and his father loved him so, that it was no trouble—no trouble. And there is your father at the door!"

She hurried out to meet him, and little Bob in his comforter—he had need of it, poor fellow—came in. His tea was ready for him on the hob, and they all tried who should help him to it most. Then the two young Cratchits got upon his knees, and laid, each child, a little cheek against his face, as if they said, "Don't mind it, father. Don't be grieved!"

Bob was very cheerful with them, and spoke pleasantly to all the family. He looked at the work upon the table, and praised the industry and speed of Mrs. Cratchit and the girls. They would be done long before Sunday, he said.

"Sunday! You went today, then, Robert?" said his wife.

"Yes, my dear," returned Bob. "I wish you could have gone. It would have done you good to see how green a place it is. But you'll see it often. I promised him that I would walk there on a Sunday. My little, little child!" cried Bob. "My little child!"

He broke down all at once. He couldn't help it. If he could have helped it, he and his child would have been farther apart, perhaps, than they were.

He left the room, and went upstairs into the room above, which was lighted cheerfully, and hung with Christmas. There was a chair set close beside the child, and there were signs of someone having been there lately. Poor Bob sat down in it, and when he had thought a little and composed himself he kissed the little face. He was reconciled to what had happened, and went down again quite happy.

They drew about the fire and talked, the girls and mother working still. Bob told them of the extraordinary kindness of Mr. Scrooge's nephew, whom he had scarcely seen but once, and who, meeting him in the street that day, and seeing that he looked a little—"just a little down, you know," said Bob, inquired what had happened to distress him. "On which," said Bob, "for he is the pleasantest-spoken gentleman you ever heard, I told him. 'I am heartily sorry for it, Mr. Cratchit,' he said, 'and heartily sorry for your good wife.' By the by, how he ever knew *that*, I don't know."

"Knew what, my dear?"

"Why, that you were a good wife," replied Bob.

"Everybody knows that," said Peter.

"Very well observed, my boy!" cried Bob. "I hope they do. 'Heartily sorry,' he said, 'for your good wife. If I can be of service to you in any way,' he said, giving me his card, 'that's where I live. Pray come to me.' No it wasn't," cried Bob, "for the sake of anything he might be able to do for us, so much as for his kind way, that this was quite delightful. It really seemed as if he had known our

Tiny Tim, and felt with us."

"I'm sure he's a good soul!" said Mrs. Cratchit.

"You would be sure of it, my dear," returned Bob, "if you saw and spoke to him. I shouldn't be at all surprised—mark what I say!—if he got Peter a better situation."

"Only hear that, Peter," said Mrs. Cratchit.

"And then," cried one of the girls, "Peter will be keeping company with someone, and setting up for himself."

"Get along with you!" retorted Peter, grinning.

"It's just as likely as not," said Bob, "one of these days, though there's plenty of time for that, my dear. But, however and whenever we part from one another, I am sure we shall none of us forget poor Tiny Tim—shall we?—or this first parting that there was among us?"

"Never, father!" cried they all.

"And I know," said Bob—"I know, my dears, that when we recollect how patient and how mild he was, although he was a little, little child, we shall not quarrel easily among ourselves, and forget poor Tiny Tim in doing it."

"No, never, father!" they all cried again.

"I am very happy," said little Bob—"I am very happy!"

Mrs. Cratchit kissed him, his daughters kissed him, the two young Cratchits kissed him, and Peter and himself shook hands. Spirit of Tiny Tim, thy childish essence was from God!

"Specter," said Scrooge, "something informs me that our parting moment is at hand. I know it, but I know not how. Tell me what man that was whom we saw lying dead."

The Ghost of Christmas Yet to Come conveyed him, as before—though at a different time, he thought; indeed, there seemed no order in these latter visions, save that they were in the Future—into the resorts of businessmen, but showed him not himself. Indeed, the Spirit did not stay for anything, but went straight on, as to the end just now desired, until besought by Scrooge to tarry for a moment.

"This court," said Scrooge, "through which we hurry now is where my place of occupation is, and has been for a length of time. I see the house. Let me behold what I shall be, in days to come!"

The Spirit stopped; the hand was pointed elsewhere.

"The house is yonder," Scrooge exclaimed. "Why do you point away?"

The inexorable finger underwent no change.

Scrooge hastened to the window of his office, and looked in. It was an office still, but not his. The furniture was not the same, and the figure in the chair was not himself. The Phantom pointed as before.

He joined it once again, and, wondering why and whither he had gone, accompanied it until they reached an iron gate. He paused to look round before entering.

A churchyard. Here, then, the wretched man whose name he had now to learn lay underneath the ground. It was a worthy place. Walled in by houses, overrun by grass and weeds, the growth of vegetation's death, not life; choked up with too much burying, fat with repleted appetite. A worthy place!

The Spirit stood among the graves, and pointed down to One. He advanced toward it, trembling. The Phantom was exactly as it had been, but he dreaded that he saw new meaning in its solemn shape.

"Before I draw nearer to that stone to which you point," said Scrooge, "answer me one question. Are these the shadows of the things that Will be or are they shadows of the things that May be, only?"

Still the Ghost pointed downward to the grave by which it stood.

"Men's courses will foreshadow certain ends, to which, if persevered in, they must lead," said Scrooge. "But if the courses be departed from, the ends will change. Say it is thus with what you show me!"

The Spirit was immovable as ever.

Scrooge crept toward it, trembling as he went; and following the finger, read upon the stone of the neglected grave his own name, EBENEZER SCROOGE.

"Am *I* that man who lay upon the bed?" he

cried, upon his knees.

The finger pointed from the grave to him, and back again.

"No, Spirit! Oh, no, no!"

The finger still was there.

"Spirit!" he cried, tight clutching at its robe, "hear me! I am not the man I was. I will not be the man I must have been but for this intercourse. Why show me this, if I am past all hope?"

For the first time the hand appeared to shake.

"Good Spirit," he pursued, as down upon the ground he fell before it, "your nature intercedes for me, and pities me. Assure me that I yet may change these shadows you have shown me, by an altered life!"

The kind hand trembled.

"I will honor Christmas in my heart, and try to keep it all the year. I will live in the Past, Present, and the Future. The Spirits of all Three shall strive within me. I will not shut out the lessons that they teach. Oh, tell me I may sponge away the writing on this stone!"

In his agony he caught the spectral hand. It sought to free itself, but he was strong in his entreaty, and detained it. The Spirit, stronger yet, repulsed him.

Holding up his hands in a last prayer to have his fate reversed, he saw an alteration in the Phantom's hood and dress. It shrunk, collapsed, and dwindled down into a bedpost.

Stave Five
The End of It

Yes! And the bedpost was his own. The bed was his own, the room was his own. Best and happiest of all, the Time before him was his own, to make amends in!

"I will live in the Past, the Present, and the Future!" Scrooge repeated, as he scrambled out of the bed. "The Spirits of all Three shall strive within me. O Jacob Marley! Heaven and the Christmas-time be praised for this! I say it on my knees, old Jacob, on my knees!"

He was so fluttered and so glowing with his good intentions, that his broken voice would scarcely answer to his call. He had been sobbing violently in his conflict with the Spirit, and his face was wet with tears.

"They are not torn down," cried Scrooge,

folding one of his bed-curtains in his arms—"they are not torn down rings and all. They are here—I am here—the shadows of the things that would have been may be dispelled. They will be. I know they will!"

His hands were busy with his garments all this time; turning them inside out, putting them on upside down, tearing them, mislaying them, making them parties to every kind of extravagance.

"I don't know what to do!" cried Scrooge, laughing and crying in the same breath, and making a perfect Laocoön of himself with his stockings. "I am as light as a feather, I am as happy as an angel, I am as merry as a schoolboy. I am as giddy as a drunken man. A Merry Christmas to everybody! A Happy New Year to all the world! Hallo here! Whoop! Hallo!"

He had frisked into the sitting room, and was now standing there, perfectly winded.

"There's the saucepan that the gruel was in!" cried Scrooge, starting off again, and going round the fireplace. "There's the door by which the Ghost of Jacob Marley entered! There's the corner where the Ghost of Christmas Present sat! There's the window where I saw the wandering Spirits! It's all right, it's all true, it all happened. Ha, ha, ha!"

Really, for a man who had been out of practice for so many years, it was a splendid laugh, a most illustrious laugh. The father of a long, long line of brilliant laughs!

"I don't know what day of the month it is," said Scrooge. "I don't know how long I have been among the Spirits. I don't know anything. I'm quite a baby. Never mind. I don't care. I'd rather be a baby. Hallo! Whoop! Hallo here!"

He was checked in his transports by the churches ringing out the lustiest peals he had ever heard. Clash, clash, hammer; ding, dong, bell! Bell, dong, ding; hammer, clang, clash! Oh, glorious, glorious!

Running to the window, he opened it, and put out his head. No fog, no mist; clear, bright, jovial, stirring, cold; cold, piping for the blood to dance to; golden sunlight; heavenly sky; sweet fresh air; merry bells. Oh, glorious! Glorious!

"What's today?" cried Scrooge, calling downward to a boy in Sunday clothes, who perhaps had loitered in to look about him.

"Eh?" returned the boy, with all his might of wonder.

"What's today, my fine fellow?" said Scrooge.

"Today!" replied the boy. "Why, *Christmas Day.*"

"It's Christmas Day!" said Scrooge to himself. "I haven't missed it. The Spirits have done it all one night. They can do anything they lik course they can. Of course they can. Hallo fellow!"

"Hallo!" returned the boy.

"Do you know the poulterer's, in the next street but one, at the corner?" Scrooge inquired.

"I should hope I did," replied the lad.

"An intelligent boy!" said Scrooge. "A remarkable boy! Do you know whether they've sold the prize Turkey that was hanging up there?—Not the little prize Turkey, the big one?"

"What, the one as big as me?" returned the boy.

"What a delightful boy!" said Scrooge. "It's a pleasure to talk to him. Yes, my buck!"

"It's hanging there now," replied the boy.

"Is it?" said Scrooge. "Go and buy it."

"Walk-ER!" exclaimed the boy.

"No, no," said Scrooge. "I am in earnest. Go and buy it, and tell 'em to bring it here, that I may give them the directions where to take it. Come back with the man, and I'll give you a shilling. Come back with him in less than five minutes and I'll give you half a crown!"

The boy was off like a shot. He must have had a ⌐ l at a trigger who could have got a shot ⌐ ast.

⌐ it to Bob Cratchit's," whispered ⌐ ng his hands, and splitting with a ⌐ 'n't know who sends it. It's twice ⌐ im. Joe Miller never made such a ⌐ to Bob's will be!"

⌐ ch he wrote the address was not ⌐ rite it he did, somehow, and went downstairs to open the street door, ready for the coming of the poulterer's man. As he stood there, waiting his arrival, the knocker caught his eye.

"I shall love it as long as I live!" cried Scrooge, patting it with his hand. "I scarcely ever looked at it before. What an honest expression it has in its face! It's a wonderful knocker!—Here's the Turkey. Hallo! How are you? Merry Christmas!"

It *was* a Turkey! He never could have stood upon his legs, that bird. He would have snapped 'em short off in a minute, like sticks of sealing-wax.

"Why, it's impossible to carry that to Camden Town," said Scrooge. "You must have a cab."

The chuckle with which he said this, and the chuckle with which he paid for the Turkey, and the chuckle with which he paid for the cab, and the chuckle with which he recompensed the boy, were only to be exceeded by the chuckle with which he sat down breathless in his chair again, and chuckled till he cried.

Shaving was not an easy task, for his hand continued to shake very much and shaving requires attention, even when you don't dance while you are at it. But if he had cut the end of his nose off, he would have put a piece of sticki plaster over it, and been quite satisfied.

He dressed himself "all in his best," a got out into the streets. The people w time pouring forth, as he had seen them with the Ghost of Christmas Present; and walking with his hands behind him, Scrooge regarded everyone with a delighted smile. He looked so irresistibly pleasant, in a word, that three or four good-humored fellows said, "Good morning, sir! A Merry Christmas to you!" and Scrooge said often afterward, that of all the blithe sounds he had ever heard, those were the blithest in his ears.

He had not gone far, when, coming on toward him he beheld the portly gentleman who had walked into his counting-house the day before, and said, "Scrooge and Marley's, I believe?" It sent a pang across his heart to think how this old gentleman would look upon him when they met, but he knew what path lay straight before him, and he took it.

"My dear sir," said Scrooge, quickening his pace, and taking the old gentleman by both his hands, "how do you do? I hope you succeeded ~~yesterday~~. It was very kind of you. A Merry ~~Christmas t~~o you, sir!"

~~"Mr. Scro~~oge?"

~~"Yes," said~~ Scrooge. "That is my name, and I ~~fear it may not~~ be pleasant to you. Allow me to ask ~~your pardon. An~~d will you have the goodness—"

~~Here Scrooge wh~~ispered in his ear.

~~"Lord bless me!~~" cried the gentleman, as if his ~~breath were taken a~~way. "My dear Mr. Scrooge, are

"If you please," said Scrooge. "Not a farthing less. A great many back payments are included in it, I assure you. Will you do me that favor?"

"My dear sir," said the other, shaking hands with him, "I don't know what to say to such munifi—"

"Don't say anything, please," retorted Scrooge. "Come and see me. Will you come and see me?"

"I will!" cried the old gentleman. And it was clear he meant to do it.

"Thankee," said Scrooge. "I am much obliged to you. I thank you fifty times. Bless you!"

He went to church, and walked about the streets, and watched the people hurrying to and fro, and patted the children on the head, and questioned beggars, and looked down into the kitchens of houses, and up to the windows, and found that everything could yield him pleasure. He had never dreamed that any walk—that anything—could give him so much happiness. In the afternoon, he turned his steps toward his nephew's house.

He passed the door a dozen times before he had the courage to go up and knock. But he made a dash, and did it.

"Is your master at home, my dear?" said Scrooge to the girl. Nice girl! Very.

"Yes, sir."

"Where is he, my love?" said Scrooge.

"He's in the dining room, sir, along with

mistress. I'll show you upstairs, if you please."

"Thankee. He knows me," said Scrooge, with his hand already on the dining-room lock. "I'll go in here, my dear."

He turned it gently, and sidled his face in, round the door. They were looking at the table (which was spread out in great array); for these young housekeepers are always nervous on such points, and like to see that everything is right.

"Fred!" said Scrooge.

Dear heart alive, how his niece by marriage started! Scrooge had forgotten, for the moment, about her sitting in the corner with the footstool, or he wouldn't have done it, on any account.

"Why, bless my soul!" cried Fred, "who's that?"

"It's I. Your Uncle Scrooge. I have come to dinner. Will you let me in, Fred?"

Let him in! It is a mercy he didn't shake his arm off. He was at home in five minutes. Nothing could be heartier. His niece looked just the same. So did Topper, when *he* came. So did the plump sister, when *she* came. So did everyone, when *they* came. Wonderful party, wonderful games, wonderful unanimity, won-der-ful happiness!

But he was early at the office next morning. Oh, he was early there! If he could only be there first, and catch Bob Cratchit coming late! That was the thing he had set his heart upon.

And he did it, yes, he did! The clock struck nine. No Bob. A quarter past. No Bob. He was full eighteen minutes and a half behind his time. Scrooge sat with his door wide open, that he might see him come into the tank.

His hat was off before he opened the door, his comforter, too. He was on his stool in a jiffy driving away with his pen, as if he were trying to overtake nine o'clock.

"Hallo!" growled Scrooge, in his accustomed voice as near as he could feign it. "What do you mean by coming here at this time of day?"

"I am very sorry, sir," said Bob. "I *am* behind my time."

"You are?" repeated Scrooge. "Yes. I think you are. Step this way, sir, if you please."

"It's only once a year, sir," pleaded Bob, appearing from the tank. "It shall not be repeated. I was making rather merry yesterday, sir."

"Now, I'll tell you what, my friend," said Scrooge, "I am not going to stand this sort of thing any longer. And therefore," he continued, leaping from his stool, and giving Bob such a dig in the waistcoat that he staggered back into the tank again—"and therefore, I am about to raise your salary!"

Bob trembled, and got a little nearer to the ruler. He had a momentary idea of knocking Scrooge down with it, holding him, and calling to the people in the court for help and a strait-waistcoat.

"A Merry Christmas, Bob!" said Scrooge, with an earnestness that could not be mistaken, as he clapped him on the back. "A merrier Christmas, Bob, my good fellow, than I have given you for many a year! I'll raise your salary, and endeavor to assist your struggling family, and we will discuss your affairs this very afternoon, over a Christmas bowl of smoking bishop, Bob! Make up the fires, and buy another coal-scuttle before you dot another *i*, Bob Cratchit!"

Scrooge was better than his word. He did it all, and infinitely more; and to Tiny Tim, who did NOT die, he was a second father. He became as good a friend, as good a master, and as good a man as the good old City knew, or any other good old city, town, or borough in the good old world. Some people laughed to see the alteration in him, but he let them laugh, and little heeded them, for he was wise enough to know that nothing ever happened on this globe, for good, at which some people did not have their fill of laughter in the outset; and knowing that such as these would be blind anyway, he thought it quite as well that they should wrinkle up their eyes in grins, as have the malady in less attractive forms. His own heart laughed, and that was quite enough for him.

He had no further intercourse with Spirits, but lived upon the Total Abstinence Principle ever afterward; and it was always said of him, that he knew how to keep Christmas well, if any man alive possessed the knowledge. May that be truly said of us, and all of us! And so, as Tiny Tim observed, God Bless Us, Every One!

JEWEL thieves

battle of
the brightest

by Hope McLean

Scholastic Inc.

*For Hana and Ava,
two book-loving sisters who would make
a great addition to any quiz bowl team.*

ISBN 978-0-545-48292-9

12 11 10 9 8 7 6 5 4 3   13 14 15 16 17/0

Printed in the U.S.A.   40
First printing, January 2013

Book design by Natalie C. Sousa

Chapter One

"This is a crime against fashion!" Lili Higashida shrieked, strapping on a thick black vest.

"It's not supposed to be fashionable," countered her friend Erin Fischer.

"Are you sure this doesn't hurt?" asked Jasmine Johnson, nervously looking around the equipment room, where dozens of laser guns hung from the wall. "I mean, I know it's just lasers, but it looks pretty dangerous."

"Well, once I tripped over my shoelace and skinned my knee," Erin admitted. "But that's about as dangerous as it gets. Actually, this is a miracle of modern technology. See?" Erin pointed to her vest. "The lights on the shoulders show what color team you're on. These ports on your back and chest will register when someone makes a hit. The lights will go off for ten seconds, and when they're on again you know it's okay to shoot."

Lili sighed. "Why couldn't you have chosen something normal, Erin?"

Willow Albern came to Erin's defense. "Lili, this whole 'friendship checkup' thing was your idea, anyway," she pointed out. "And when it was your turn to choose the activity we went to the art exhibit."

"Yeah, well, that was awesome!" Lili said.

Willow rolled her eyes. "It was just a bunch of squiggles. My little brothers can do better than that."

Lili frowned. "Anyway, we wouldn't have to do these friendship checkups if you and Jasmine would just play nice."

Jasmine and Willow looked uncomfortable. Even though they'd been friends since they were little, they had recently been arguing with each other a lot. Jasmine had become so upset that she briefly quit the Jewels, the middle school quiz bowl team the girls competed on together.

"We *are* playing nice," Jasmine insisted. "So don't you think a game of laser tag defeats the whole purpose of that?"

"No, because the purpose of this is fun," Erin said cheerfully.

It was Friday night, and the Laser Emporium in the Hallytown Mall was filling up fast with other players. One mom had brought three young kids into the equipment room, and five teenage boys were suiting up, too.

Another boy wearing a red Laser Emporium T-shirt entered the room.

"Hi, my name is Chip," he said in a bored voice. "I need to tell you the rules now, so pay attention."

Chip explained how the vests worked, just like Erin had. Then he outlined the rules of the game.

"You get fifty points every time you hit someone in the back of the vest, a hundred points if you hit the front," he said. "The targets in each base are worth three hundred points each. There are also hidden targets on the course for bonus points."

"Where are they?" one of the little kids asked.

"I said they're *hidden*," Chip explained, rolling his eyes. "Does anyone else have questions?"

"I do, but I'm afraid to ask," Jasmine whispered to Willow.

"Don't worry," Willow whispered back. "There are lots of places to hide on the course."

"Oh yeah, the most important thing is no running," Chip added. "Now please proceed to the red door."

The teenage boys rushed to the red starting gate, practically knocking over the girls. Jasmine nervously wiped her palms on her leggings.

"How about I just watch?" she asked.

Willow grabbed her hand. "Just lie low, and you'll be fine."

Chip opened the door to a black cavernous room decorated to look like the surface of a strange planet. Large fluorescent orange rocks dotted the landscape, and the walls were painted to show a purple-pink sky with three moons floating in it. Special black lights lit up the space, so the rocks and the sky glowed in the dark. When the girls walked onto the course, it was hard to focus on anything except the colored lights on their own vests.

"The game will begin in fifteen seconds," Chip instructed. One of the teenage boys started to speed away, but Chip stopped him with a booming command. "NO RUNNING!"

Then a robotic voice started to count down over the speakers. "Fifteen . . . fourteen . . . thirteen . . ."

The little kids started trotting away, with their mom hurrying to keep up. The teenagers weren't running, exactly, but they, too, were moving pretty fast.

"Oh my gosh. What do we do? Where do we go?" Lili fretted.

"Stick with me," Erin said. "I got your back."

Erin took off after the teenage boys, with Lili following nervously behind her. Jasmine wanted to stick with Willow, her super-athletic friend, but she, too, was already racing across the course.

Panicked, Jasmine found the biggest rock in the farthest corner and hid behind it.

"Three . . . two . . . one . . . commence play!"

The teen boys all went after one another, darting among the rocks and shooting blast after blast. Erin and Willow snuck up on all of them, scoring points by shooting quickly and then zipping away.

Distracted by her conquests, Erin forgot her promise to watch over Lili, who was soon surrounded by the three younger kids.

Pew! Pew! Pew! They barraged Lili with shots, and the lights on her vest went dead. She shrieked with laughter, despite herself.

"Aaaaaah! They got me! They got me!"

Behind the rock, Jasmine held her breath, hoping nobody would notice her. From the corner of her eye she saw a round red light on a rock hanging down from the ceiling.

Remembering what Chip had said about targets, she took aim and fired at the light. It flashed and then died out.

"Woo hoo!" Jasmine yelled, and then covered her mouth with her hand, but it was too late. One of the older boys heard and walked up to her, shooting her in the back. But Jasmine didn't mind so much. She used her ten seconds to look for another hiding place — and another target.

It seemed like the battle had just begun when the robot voice came over the speakers again.

"Game ending in ten . . . nine . . . eight . . ."

Everyone except Jasmine was zipping around the field like crazy, walking as fast as they could without actually running. Willow and Erin were chasing each other now, laughing. Lili hid, waiting until the three little kids walked past, and then she jumped out.

Pew! Pew! Pew! She hit all three.

"Revenge!" she cried happily, raising her fist in the air.

Jasmine carefully made her way around the perimeter, hitting every target she could find. Then the count was over, and Chip entered the course.

"Okay! Everybody out!"

After they took off their vests and turned in their laser guns, they went up to the front counter, where each player got a printed sheet showing their score.

"Yes!" Erin cried. "I hit that one guy twelve times."

Then she frowned and turned to Willow. "You hit me eight times? Seriously?"

Willow shrugged. "It's all about the points!"

"My score is pathetic," Lili said. "But I have to admit, it was fun."

"I got eleven hundred points," Jasmine said. "Is that good?"

Erin and Willow both stared at Jasmine.

"Are you serious?" Erin asked. "That's awesome! How did you get all those points?"

Jasmine shrugged. "I just aimed at the targets, that's all."

Erin shook her head. "It's always the quiet ones, isn't it?"

"Why? What score did you get?" Jasmine asked.

"Never mind!" Erin and Willow said together, and then they laughed.

Lili put her hands on her hips. "Come on, guys. Friendship night isn't supposed to be competitive."

"Is anyone else hungry?" Erin asked, quickly changing the subject.

"I could go for some pizza," Jasmine answered.

They made their way across the mall to their favorite pizza place, Mario's. It wasn't part of the food court, but a little restaurant all on its own.

"One large plain and four waters?" Willow asked her friends.

Erin checked the pockets of her jeans. "Four bucks each, right? Got it." She handed Willow the cash. "Lili and I will find a table for us."

A few minutes later they were seated at one of the metal tables, biting into slices of hot pizza.

"Sooo good," Erin said, taking in a mouthful at the same time.

Lili giggled. "Erin, you've got cheese all over your chin."

Erin reached for the napkin holder, but it was empty. Willow noticed and flagged down the bus boy, who came back a minute later with a holder stuffed with new napkins. The girls each took one.

"Well, that was fun," Lili said. "It's nice to take a break from quiz bowl practice once in a while, isn't it?"

Jasmine nodded. "Although we need to keep up with practices. We've got Nationals in a few weeks. I can't believe we qualified!"

Willow nodded. "Especially since this is the first year that Martha Washington School has had a team in ages."

"Well, anyway, we still need to practice," Jasmine said. "I bet the Rivals are training right now."

"I bet they practice in their sleep!" Erin joked.

"Except when they're busy stealing jewels," Lili added.

The Rivals, the academic team from Atkinson Preparatory School, were the stars of the middle school quiz bowl scene. They also happened to be jewel thieves.

Willow groaned. "Don't remind me. They're probably plotting how to steal the sapphire at this very moment, if they don't have it already."

"That's what bugs me," Erin said. "For all we know, they could have all four jewels by now, and have already figured out the clues."

The four friends had gotten involved with the Rivals' jewel thefts when the Martha Washington ruby was stolen, and Jasmine was the main suspect. Then they discovered a letter written by Martha Washington herself that said there were *four* special jewels: a ruby, a diamond, an emerald, and a sapphire. According to what the girls had learned, each jewel held a clue etched on the back that led to some kind of important thing — a treasure, maybe. At least, that's what they hoped.

The Jewels couldn't get the ruby back from the Rivals, but they did prevent them from stealing the diamond — for a while. Unfortunately, the Rivals stole it back. And then they went after the emerald, which was owned by a wealthy socialite and TV star named Derrica Girard. Jasmine had held it in her hands, but only for a few seconds. It was with the Rivals now.

"Don't forget what Derrica said," Jasmine reminded them. "She's heard that Arthur Atkinson has been asking around about a sapphire. So I don't think they have it yet."

Arthur Atkinson, the director of Atkinson Preparatory School, had been helping the Rivals steal jewels all along.

"Then we can find it first," Willow said.

Erin nodded. "We tracked down the diamond all on our own. I bet we could find the sapphire."

Jasmine frowned. "Principal Frederickson is watching our every move these days," she said. "She doesn't want us looking for the jewels, and I certainly don't want to get in trouble with her."

"She doesn't have to find out," Erin said, smiling, her mouth ringed with tomato sauce.

Jasmine shook her head. "Napkin, Erin!"

Erin reached for a napkin, but when she held it up to her face she stopped. She wasn't holding a napkin at all. It was a piece of lined yellow paper, folded into a square.

"No way!" Erin cried. "It's another secret message!"

Chapter Two

The girls sat in silence for a second as they gazed at the yellow notebook paper, their eyes wide. It wasn't the first time they had seen a note like this. The same kind of paper had been used by a mysterious helper who had left them clues to help find the diamond.

Erin eagerly began to unfold the paper, but Willow put a finger to her lips and raised an eyebrow. Her gaze scanned the room, looking for whoever could have planted the note. The other Jewels joined in, checking out the room. But nothing — and no one — seemed suspicious. When the busboy walked by, Willow stopped him.

"Excuse me," she asked. "Where do you get the napkins to refill the dispensers?"

He wiped his hands on his apron as he shrugged. "From the big cardboard boxes in the closet. They're not anything fancy."

"Any idea how this could have gotten mixed in with them?" Erin asked, holding up the paper.

The boy sighed as he brushed his shaggy brown hair out of his eyes.

"If you've got a complaint, you gotta tell the manager." He shuffled away quickly before they could ask him anything else, clearly not wanting to get into any trouble.

Lili glanced at her phone. "My mom will be here any second to pick us up," she said. "Let's bring the note back to my house and we'll analyze it there."

After getting a ride to Lili's house from Mrs. Higashida, the girls rushed upstairs to Lili's bedroom. Erin felt like the note was burning a hole in her pocket — she couldn't wait to open and read it!

Lili's bed was piled with sketchbooks, pieces of fabric, plastic gems, and other items from her craft kit.

"So sorry!" Lili hurriedly grabbed a handful of stuff and shoved it into her closet. Jasmine and Willow sat on the bed, and Erin flopped onto the fluffy rug on the floor, clutching the note in her hand.

"Read!" Jasmine cried eagerly, her eyes shining.

Erin unfolded the paper and theatrically cleared her throat. Lili giggled as she sat down next to Erin on the rug.

"Come on," Willow pleaded impatiently.

Erin read the note out loud: " 'We shall meet when the value of seven cubed plus the number of times per month the moon orbits the Earth, adding the year the ceiling of the Sistine Chapel was completed, divided by the number of James Madison. Subtract two. Next add one hundred. Then find me in the place that tinkers are dying to get into but never leave.' "

"Huh?" Lili asked with a frown.

"It's a riddle," Jasmine said. She pulled out a mini notebook from her bag and a small purple pen. "We need to figure it out."

Willow reached off the bed and grabbed the note from Erin's hand. "Hey — help yourself, why don't you!" Erin cried.

"Sorry." Willow grinned sheepishly. "Do you mind?"

Erin rolled her eyes. "Fine, have at it."

"We just had a friendship checkup!" Lili yelled. "Everyone behave."

"Or else Lili will make us use finger-paints and sock puppets to get in touch with our inner feelings," Erin said with a grin.

Lili's eyes got big. "Hey, that gives me an idea!" Willow groaned.

"Guys, enough! Let's focus," Jasmine said sharply as she clicked the tip of her pen. "Willow, read it again slowly."

Willow began. " 'We shall meet when the value of seven cubed —' " She shut her eyes as she ran the calculations in her head. "Let's see, that's seven to the third power or . . . three hundred and forty-three!" she said confidently in the same tone of voice she used when answering a quiz bowl question.

"Okay, so far we have three forty-three," Jasmine said as she jotted the number in her notebook. "What's next?"

13

Willow continued. "'Plus the number of times per month the moon orbits the Earth.'"

Jasmine snorted. "Simple. If this is a riddle, it's a really easy one. The answer is one," she said as she wrote it down.

"So right now we have three forty-four," Lili said. "What's next?"

"'Adding the year the ceiling of the Sistine Chapel was completed,'" Willow read.

Lili's eyes glowed. "Michelangelo, what a genius! Did you know that it's a myth he painted the ceiling of the Sistine Chapel while lying on his back? He was so super-smart, he invented this totally innovative scaffolding system instead. There are more than three hundred painted figures on that ceiling!" Lili gazed into the distance with a dreamy look in her eyes.

"Um, Lili?" Erin nudged her friend gently. "That's really great and all, but do you know when he finished painting it?"

Lili shook her head as her eyes drifted back to her friends. "Oh yeah!" she giggled. "Sorry. 1512."

Jasmine wrote in her notebook. "That makes the total 1856." She frowned. "How can we meet someone in 1856?"

"Last time I checked I don't own a time machine!" Erin said. "But, man, how awesome would that be?!"

Willow got that stern look on her face, the one she always made when the conversation began to drift off topic. "We're not finished," she said seriously before continuing to read. " 'Divided by the number of James Madison.' "

Lili looked confused. "James Madison is a person, not a number."

"Ha! He is a person who will always be known by one number, and that's the number four," Erin said triumphantly. "Madison was the fourth president of the United States. Whether you look him up in an encyclopedia or online, that's the first thing you'll find out about him."

The others nodded their heads. "Let's keep going and see what we come up with," Lili suggested. "We can always go back and try again if the final answer doesn't make any sense."

Jasmine quickly scribbled. "So that brings us to four hundred sixty-four."

Willow scanned the yellow note. "So next we subtract two."

"Four sixty-two." Jasmine shook her head. "If we add one hundred, that makes five sixty-two. Okay, it's still not making much sense."

"The next part says, 'Then find me in the place that tinkers are dying to get into but never leave,'" Willow read. "This next part of the clue tells us *where* to meet. The first part is *when*."

"Let's focus on the *when* now," Jasmine said. "We have the number five hundred and sixty-two. It can't be a time, and it doesn't look like military time, either."

Lili was thinking hard as her gaze wandered aimlessly around her room. Her eyes landed on the calendar hanging from her wall. Suddenly, she jumped up and grabbed it.

"I think I'm on to something," she said excitedly to the others. "Look," she said as she pointed at today's date. "Today is April thirtieth. Can I see your notebook, Jasmine?" Jasmine nodded and handed the pen and book to Lili. "Written out, the date looks like this." She wrote *4/30* in the notebook and held it up.

"So five-six-two could be a date — like May sixth?" Erin suggested. "But what does the two mean? It can't be the year."

Willow stood up, her eyes shining. "No, but it could be the time."

"Yes!" Erin snapped her fingers. "May sixth at two o'clock. That's next Saturday!"

Willow rubbed her chin with her hand. "But is it p.m. or a.m.?"

"No way am I meeting a stranger at two a.m.," Jasmine said fiercely.

Willow agreed. "That's so not safe. Let's assume that it's two in the afternoon. Now, let's try to figure out where. 'Find me in the place that tinkers are dying to get into but never leave,'" she read.

"Elan's Couture!" Lili cried, naming a fancy boutique the girls had once visited. Everyone looked at her strangely.

"Not the time to be thinking of fashion, Lili," Willow said.

"No!" Lili shook her head, her shiny black hair swinging around her face. "Elan's Couture is on Tinker Street!"

Tinker Street was located in the historic section of River Park, a nearby town.

"That's right!" Jasmine said. "But what near there would be a place that tinkers are dying to get into but never leave?"

Erin gasped. "I got it!" she said triumphantly. "It's the Tinker Street Historical Cemetery. It's really old. I've gone there to do research before."

Lili opened her laptop and began to type. "It says the hours are eight a.m. to five p.m."

"Then the note *must* mean two p.m.," Willow said.

"That's good." Lili shivered. "There is no way I'm going to a cemetery in the middle of the night. In fact, even the thought of going in broad daylight creeps me out a little bit."

"Don't worry, Lili." Erin put an arm around her friend. "It's a busy place. There are a lot of tourists hanging around. They even do walking tours with guides dressed in period costumes. It's not spooky at all."

Jasmine finished writing. "So to sum up, we believe the Riddler is asking us to meet him or her at the Tinker Street Historical Cemetery at two p.m. next Saturday, May sixth."

They all nodded in agreement.

"I find something else interesting about this note," Jasmine said. "It's like each part of the riddle was designed for one of us."

On their quiz bowl team, each member had an area of expertise. Erin handled the history questions, Jasmine took the science section, Willow buzzed in on the math problems, and Lili managed the arts and literature topics.

"Maybe it's all an elaborate plan by Ms. Keatley to get us to study for quiz bowl," Erin joked. Ms. Keatley was the Jewels' quiz bowl advisor and a history teacher at Martha Washington School.

"Whoever sent this note knows us pretty well," Jasmine said thoughtfully. "I can't wait to find out who it is!"

That next Saturday, the girls all piled into Mrs. Higashida's car.

"Tinker Street again?" she chuckled as she shook her head. "You girls do have expensive tastes." The exclusive shops located on the street were known to be a bit on the pricey side.

"Window shopping is totally free!" Erin said, but Jasmine sighed. She loved to look at the glittering gems on display in the jewelry shop windows. She dreamed about owning her own rare gem collection one day.

"But we'll spend most of our time touring the old cemetery this afternoon," Lili added.

Mrs. Higashida pulled into the parking garage. As they left the car, she reminded them to stay together, before heading off to meet a friend on Tinker Street for lunch.

The girls traveled down the cobblestone sidewalk, passing pretty, old brick buildings as they walked. They wore hoodies and sweaters as it was still a bit cool in late spring, but the shining sun high in the bright blue sky was warming everything up.

"It's one forty-five." Willow glanced at her phone. "I want us to be a few minutes early."

"We're almost there," Erin said. "It's right at the end of the block on the left."

The block ended and the girls found themselves standing in front of a tall black gate, which was attached to a black picket fence that encircled the area. Although it was a sunny day, the numerous trees growing throughout the cemetery blocked out the sunlight, filling it with a spooky shade of gray. Old, crooked tombstones jutted out from the ground. The girls spotted several angel statues here and there, some weeping.

Lili shivered. "Maybe we're making a mistake," she whispered.

Erin grabbed her hand. "Don't be nervous."

A woman dressed in a Revolutionary-era costume smiled at them. "Would you like a tour? The next one starts at two."

"No, thank you," Willow answered. "But do you have a map?"

"Yes, of course! Here you go," she said as she handed one to Willow, who took out a dollar from her bag and placed it in the Plexiglas donation box.

"Thank you. Enjoy!" The woman smiled at them as they walked into the old graveyard. "But watch your step. There are some fallen tombstones and tree roots that are easy to trip over."

The darkness seemed to swallow them up as they stepped inside and began strolling down the main path. Erin eagerly began reading the tombstones they passed. Some of the really old ones had skulls and crossbones etched into them.

"Very gothic," Jasmine remarked.

"If you like gothic, then check this out." Erin started to read from a tombstone dated 1789. "'All you that doth my grave pass by, as you are now, so once was I, as I am now, so you must be, prepare for death and follow me.'"

Lili let out a moan. "What time is it? I need to get out of here!"

Jasmine shook her head. "Creepy. But I wonder where we should meet our mystery person?"

The woman who had greeted them at the gate passed by with the two o'clock tour. She was talking about a skull carving on one of the headstones as a group of about ten people followed behind her. The girls scanned each one, but nobody looked familiar or suspicious.

"Let's just stay around here. It's central to the rest of the cemetery," Willow said as she consulted the map, "and we can see anyone who comes in the gate here."

The girls passed the time by reading the tombstones. "'Here lies Mary, the beloved wife of James Selman. She did much good in her life,'" Erin read.

Lili sniffed. "Awww. I should come back and bring flowers for her."

Several people passed through the gate, but they didn't pay any attention to the Jewels.

"It's after two," Willow said. "I wonder if we got the riddle wrong after all."

Erin gasped. "Rats!" she said in a loud whisper. "Of course *he* would have to show up and ruin everything." She jerked her head toward the gate, gesturing for the other girls to look.

Ryan Atkinson, the captain of the Rivals' quiz bowl team, was walking into the cemetery. A tall boy with wavy blond hair, he wore jeans and a blue shirt.

"He might scare away whoever is trying to contact us," Jasmine whispered back.

"Should we try to hide?" Lili asked, panicked.

"It's too late," Willow replied as Ryan began walking toward them. He looked directly at the Jewels and waved, giving them the smug smile they had all come to hate.

"Don't give anything away," Willow whispered to the others as Ryan strode over to them.

Willow looked Ryan right in the eyes. "Hi, Ryan," she said. "Here for the tour? You're a little late."

Ryan grinned. "I'm not here for the tour — I'm here for you. I'm the one who sent you that note, and all the others before it," he said, as the girls went silent in complete shock. "And I need you to help me steal the Atkinson sapphire."

Chapter Three

The girls were totally stunned for a moment. Erin spoke up first.

"What do you mean, *you* sent us the note?"

"It doesn't make any sense," Jasmine blurted out. "I mean, those notes in New York warned us that you were going to steal the diamond. Why would you do that to yourself?"

"We can't talk here," Ryan replied, looking around. "Why don't you follow me to Café X?"

Without waiting for an answer, he turned and began to walk out of the cemetery.

"We should follow him," Willow said. "We need to figure out what's going on."

"Are you serious?" Erin asked, folding her arms in front of her. "I am not going anywhere with that thief. He's probably leading us into a trap."

"Erin's right," Jasmine said, frowning. "We can't trust him."

"It's a public place in the middle of the day," Willow pointed out. "What can he possibly do? Aren't you curious to know what all this is about?"

Lili anxiously bit her lower lip. "I definitely am. I think we should go."

Jasmine sighed. "Me, too, I guess."

"No way," Erin said.

"If anything looks weird, we'll leave right away," Willow assured her.

Erin's eyes narrowed, and she made a low growling noise. "I am going under protest," she informed her friends.

Ryan had already left the cemetery, but they knew where Café X was. The hip coffee shop was on a corner along Tinker Street, with wide windows on the front and side. Several patrons sat at small round tables by the windows and sipped their drinks, watching people walk by.

The girls stepped inside. Ryan was beckoning to them from the back of the room. Seated with him at the rectangular table were the other three members of the Rivals' quiz bowl team: Aaron Santiago, Veronica Manasas, and Isabel Baudin.

Erin quickly turned and started to walk away. Willow grabbed her by the arm.

"Erin, where are you going?" she asked.

"Isabel's here," Erin said. "I said I would leave if I saw anything weird, remember?"

"Very funny," Willow said. "Come on, I'm even more curious now."

The girls sat down, four Jewels facing four Rivals.

"I'm glad you came," Ryan said. "I guess you probably want me to explain."

"Um, yeah!" Erin answered, annoyed.

Isabel rolled her eyes. "I told you it is ridiculous to trust them," she said in her French accent. "This is a big mistake."

"It's ridiculous to trust *us*?" Erin asked incredulously. "You guys are the jewel thieves."

Veronica turned to Isabel. "Just let him do it," she said, sounding even more annoyed than Erin. "I'm sick of this whole thing."

"Will you guys let Ryan talk, please?" Aaron interrupted.

Erin, Veronica, and Isabel got quiet.

"Okay," Ryan said. "It's like this. You know about the Atkinson sapphire, right?"

Jasmine nodded. "It belonged to your school, but then it was stolen, like, seventy years ago."

"Right," Ryan said. "So my uncle Arthur came to us one day and told us that he knew how to get it back. He said we had to find three jewels: a ruby, a diamond, and an emerald. He said that each jewel had a clue on it, and if we got all three, they would lead us to the sapphire."

"Three clues?" Willow asked. "But there are four clues, and they all lead to some kind of treasure, not the *sapphire*."

"I know," Ryan interrupted her. "You see, that's the story my uncle told us at first, and we believed him. We wanted to get the sapphire back, to restore the honor of our school."

"I just wanted to have fun," Isabel piped up.

Veronica shook her head. "Fun? Really? Because I've been miserable this whole time."

"Well, it has been kind of fun," Aaron admitted. "And I mean, we didn't think we were doing anything wrong. We really thought we were going to get the sapphire back."

"Exactly," Ryan said. "But then we started to get suspicious. Lili, remember when we bugged your pen?"

"How could I forget?" Lili asked. "That was really mean!"

"I guess it was," Ryan admitted with a sigh. "So, we were listening to you guys through the hidden microphone in your pen and we heard you talking about four clues, not three. We asked my uncle about it, and he convinced us you guys were wrong."

"That was easy to believe," Isabel remarked, and Erin glared at her.

Ryan continued his story. "But once we got the emerald, my uncle confessed that he had been lying the entire time. He admitted that the sapphire had a clue, too, and once he had all four clues, they would lead to something big."

"Did he say what it was?" Jasmine asked.

Ryan shook his head. "No. But anyway, we realized he had been using us. He said he was close to finding the sapphire and didn't need our help anymore."

"Can you imagine that?" Isabel fumed. "He just tossed us aside, like we were peasants."

"So that's why we want you to help us find the sapphire," Ryan said. "We want to find it before my uncle does."

"But why do you need our help?" Willow asked. "And why were you sending us clues to help us find the diamond? Weren't you trying to steal it for your uncle?"

"Yes," Ryan admitted. "And we had some ideas about where the diamond was in New York, but we weren't sure. So Isabel had this idea that maybe you could help us figure it out."

"Which we did," Erin said, glaring at Isabel.

"I still don't get it," Willow said. "Weren't you worried that we would get to the diamond before you?"

Ryan looked sheepish. "Honestly, we didn't think you had it in you to actually steal it," he said. "Which, technically, you didn't. You outsmarted us after *we* stole it and got it back."

"Just for a little while," Isabel interjected. "Stealing it back from you was like taking candy from a baby, as you say."

"That's because we're not lousy jewel thieves," Erin said hotly. "What you guys did was wrong."

"And now we want to make it right," Ryan said quickly. "Besides, don't you want to get your ruby back?"

The four Jewels looked at one another. This whole thing had started when the Rivals stole the Martha Washington ruby, and the girls wanted it back more than anything.

Jasmine looked suspicious. "How could we get it back if your uncle has it?"

"Once we get the sapphire and find the treasure, we can use it as leverage," Ryan said confidently. "He wants that sapphire pretty badly. He'll have to meet our demands."

"Besides, he already has the clue from the ruby," Isabel added. "That's all he really needed from it, anyway."

Willow was still full of questions. "How do you know the four jewels lead to a treasure? We've been wondering about that ourselves."

Ryan frowned. "My uncle wouldn't tell me," he said, and Willow could tell this upset him. "Uncle Arthur was always my favorite when I was a kid. It felt good to help him — made me feel important, you know? But in the end it was like he didn't care about me at all, unless I could help him."

"But we imagine that the jewels lead to something very valuable," Isabel added. "Otherwise, why would he go to all this trouble to get it?"

"Well, Martha Washington said the jewels led to something important," Erin said. "That's a fact, not a *guess*." She looked at Isabel as she emphasized that last word.

Willow nodded thoughtfully. Everything was adding up.

"So will you help us or not?" Ryan asked.

"We need to talk it over by ourselves," Jasmine said quickly. "Come on."

The four Jewels went to a table in the far corner of the café.

"So what should we do?" Lili asked.

"It's an interesting proposal," Willow admitted. "I like the idea of getting the ruby back."

"And I really like the idea of getting back at Arthur Atkinson," Jasmine said, remembering the embarrassment he had caused her.

"I can't believe you guys!" Erin said. "It is completely ridiculous to think about trusting these losers for one second. They're thieves! You heard Ryan. He used us once to find the diamond. How do we know he's not using us again now?"

Willow nodded. "I get it."

"But somehow I think Ryan is telling the truth," Jasmine added. "I can just . . . feel it."

"I think we should help them," Lili said. "I mean, I really want to know what the four jewels all lead to. And even if the Rivals are tricking us, we might be able to find out."

"I agree," Willow said. "I say let's trust them."

"And I say no way!" Erin said, shaking her head in anger. Then she stormed out of the café.

Chapter Four

Erin furiously stomped out onto the sidewalk and flopped onto a black wrought-iron bench along the street. *Have my friends all lost their minds?* she wondered. *Do they seriously want us to work with the Rivals?* As she shook her head, she felt a hand gingerly touch her on the shoulder.

"Lili," she began as she whirled around, expecting to see her friend. "There is no way I'm working with those jerks and that's that!"

But it wasn't Lili. It was Veronica! She smiled sheepishly at Erin.

"Oh," Erin said. Out of all of the Rivals, she actually liked Veronica and felt a little guilty about what she had just said. "Um, sorry, Veronica. But I don't know how we can trust you guys after everything that has happened."

Veronica let out a huge sigh and sat down next to Erin on the bench.

"I don't blame you one bit," she said, and Erin looked at her in surprise.

"I never, ever wanted to be involved in those jewel thefts," Veronica admitted. "School is really important to me. I'm proud to be on the quiz bowl team. If I could be on a team that won Nationals, I knew it would look really great on my college applications later on." Veronica frowned. "But then Ryan talked us into stealing the ruby. And then the diamond. And then the emerald. Instead of practicing for quiz bowl, we spent most of our time planning the next heist. But I was afraid to say anything. I thought they might kick me off the quiz bowl team, so I went along with it. Quiz bowl is one thing that actually makes my parents proud of me."

A memory clicked in Erin's head. "That's right! Your older sister was Miss Hallytown."

"Yes, my perfect beauty-queen sister, Amelia," Veronica said with a rueful laugh. "And I remember you have a perfect older sister, too."

Erin wrinkled her nose. "Oh, yes, the wonderful and amazing Mary Ellen."

They laughed together.

"But seriously," Veronica said, "Ryan is trying to turn things around. He is really mad at his uncle. And I feel guilty about those stolen jewels. I just want to see them returned to their rightful owners. And I know in order to do it we'll need your help."

Erin let out a deep breath. "I don't know," she said, pausing to think about it. "Hey, I really like your shirt."

Veronica had her long black hair pulled into a messy ponytail. She wore jeans and a T-shirt that had a picture of a petri dish on it that said, "When life gives you mold, make penicillin."

Veronica laughed. "Thanks. You should have seen the argument I had with my mom over it. She always wants me to wear frilly, girly stuff like Amelia does. And she's always giving me my sister's hand-me-downs."

"Veronica, I think your mom and my mom could be best friends." Erin smiled briefly before her face turned serious. "If you pinky swear to me right now that everything Ryan said is true, I will help you find the sapphire."

Veronica held up her little finger. "Pinky swear," she said solemnly. Erin linked pinkies with her and shook.

Erin stood up and then groaned. "I just remembered Isabel. How do you deal with her?"

Veronica grinned and pulled her earbuds out of her pocket. "I wear these a lot when she is talking."

They were both laughing as they walked back into Café X. The Jewels looked up at them in surprise. Erin sat down next to them as Veronica made her way back to the Rivals' table.

"So?" Lili asked hopefully.

"I'm in," Erin said. "But I say we need to be careful. I like Veronica, but I don't trust the others."

"Agreed." Willow nodded. "We'll do this, but we'll be smart. Let's go tell them."

The girls walked back to the Rivals' table and sat down.

"We will help you find the sapphire," Willow said.

"Great!" Ryan replied. "Now let's get started. First, we'll head over to Aaron's house and set up a command center. Next, we'll —"

"Whoa!" Willow put her hand in the air. "Slow down. We said we'll help, but as equal partners." She looked at her friends. "I think we'd all be more comfortable meeting at my house," she said as Erin, Jasmine, and Lili nodded their heads in agreement.

Ryan gave his signature smug smile. "But Aaron has a superfast Wi-Fi connection and a fifty-six-inch television in his bedroom so we can hook up our laptops. I'm sure you don't have those things."

"Whatever we used before, it was good enough to find the diamond for you," Willow reminded him as her eyes flashed. "It's my house or the deal is off."

"Fine," Ryan said reluctantly. "Let's head over."

As they all got up and gathered their things, Jasmine hung back to talk to Willow.

"How weird is this going to be?" Jasmine wondered. "Hanging out with the Rivals at your house?"

"I never would have seen this coming!" Willow said. "But I'm interested to see how they work together. Ryan sure is bossy."

Jasmine worked hard to keep a straight face. Willow could be a bit bossy herself at times!

Back at Willow's house, they all crammed into Willow's small but neat bedroom. The Jewels sat on the bed, while Ryan took a seat at Willow's desk and Aaron and Veronica sat on the floor.

"How quaint," Isabel sniffed as she settled into a beanbag chair.

Erin's face got red but just as she opened her mouth, Ryan took charge.

"Aaron, search for any sapphires that were sold in 1949," he barked. Aaron nodded and pulled out his laptop from his bag. "Veronica, check for any sapphires that may have been donated to a museum around that time." Veronica grabbed her smartphone for the search. "Isabel, continue cross-referencing historical events with sapphires." Isabel took her laptop out and got started right away.

The Jewels watched with their mouths open. "It's like watching soldiers," Lili whispered to Erin.

Ryan turned to the girls on the bed. "As for you, I thought maybe you could —"

35

Once again, Willow interrupted him.

"Ryan, sorry, but this is not how we work." She shook her head. "And if you're asking us for help, it means you haven't been getting anywhere on your own. I think you should try it our way."

Aaron stopped typing and looked up from his screen. "She's got a point, Ryan. All this research has gotten us nowhere."

"Fine," Ryan said as his mouth tightened. "And what exactly is *your* way?"

Lili jumped in, smiling sweetly. "Basically, we just talk!"

Ryan raised an eyebrow. "How advanced," he smirked.

Willow shot him an angry look as Jasmine spoke. "We brainstorm together," Jasmine explained. She pulled her notebook and pen out of her bag. "Let's start at the beginning. What do we know about the sapphire?"

"It was stolen from Atkinson in 1949," Isabel explained.

Jasmine began to write. "Any idea who stole it?"

Isabel shook her head. "No. There was a police investigation but no one was arrested. In fact, the police were baffled at the time. There were no leads."

"My relatives tried for years to find it," Ryan added. "To their knowledge, it has never surfaced anywhere. It's like it disappeared."

Aaron scrunched up his face as he concentrated. "I did find an old newspaper article from that year that mentioned the Memento Mori," he remembered.

"What's a Memento Mori?" Erin wondered.

"It's a super-secret club at Atkinson that still exists today," Ryan clarified. "It's only for upperclassmen, and no one knows who exactly is a member of the Memento Mori. It's very exclusive, and they're known for pulling outrageous practical jokes."

Isabel laughed. "Everyone suspects it was them who turned the swimming pool green this past St. Patrick's Day."

"Were the Memento Mori around in 1949?" Lili asked.

Aaron nodded. "According to the newspaper article, yes."

The Jewels exchanged glances. "So maybe the Memento Mori stole the sapphire as a joke!" Jasmine guessed.

"But wouldn't they have returned it?" Veronica said. "They're known for playing jokes, not stealing things."

Willow thought it over. "Since we don't have any other leads right now, it's worth looking into," she said.

Ryan shrugged. "It's impossible to get information on them. They're a highly secretive group. Even I don't have any connections to help us there."

Lili smiled. "Not a problem, Ryan. Because I think I do!"

Chapter Five

Eli gripped his flashlight tightly as he made his way through the northernmost section of the Atkinson campus, a remote spot past the sports fields. He had never been back this far, and it felt a little strange. The path he walked on, used mostly by the cross-country team, led directly into a heavily wooded area. It was a few minutes before seven thirty at night but already pretty dark out. He let out a big sigh. *Why do I let my little sister talk me into these crazy stunts?*

Over a week ago, his sister, Lili, had asked him for a favor. "Please, Eli," she begged. "We need to learn more about the Memento Mori. Rumor has it that it's a secret club only for Atkinson upperclassmen. And you're an Atkinson upperclassman!"

Eli knew all about the Jewels; the Rivals; and the ruby, diamond, emerald, and sapphire. In fact, he had helped out the Jewels many times before. He had even planted a GPS device on Ryan once. And now the Jewels were working with the Rivals! He shook his head, thinking how crazy it all was. But he had to admit, he was curious about the sapphire's location and what clue the gem might hold.

So Eli began casually dropping hints around Atkinson that he was interested in joining the Memento Mori. "I heard a rumor that the Memento Mori were responsible for turning the swimming pool green," he said loudly to his friend Zane in the crowded locker room one day after gym. "That was so cool."

He mentioned it to other friends at lunch where he was sure to be overheard. Even getting noticed by the Memento Mori was a long shot, so he was totally psyched when he discovered a mysterious note in his locker the day before:

Ithuotes   Ftesw7nt   Yomtn3ow   Ojmoi0ro

Uommgito   Wieohnhd   Anerttws   Nttrahe

But Eli couldn't make heads or tails of it. He brought it home to show Lili, who was in her room doing homework with Erin.

"I know how to read HTML, but this has me baffled," he told them. "It's letters and a few numbers, but they don't make any sense."

"I love cracking codes." Erin rubbed her hands together. "Codes were used throughout history all the time, to relay orders to soldiers in battle, to exchange messages about secret organizations. You name it, they did it all. Let me at it!"

"Hmmm." She frowned as she studied the note carefully. "It could be a code-word cipher, but I don't think it is. The words are too long. Plus we would have to guess the code word. That could take forever."

She turned to a fresh page in her notebook and rewrote the note out. "Okay," she said. "It's eight words and sixty-three letters total." She grew excited. "I think it's a simple block cipher!"

Erin drew a grid in her notebook, one with eight rows and eight columns. She began to write the letters from the note into the rows. She wrote the first letter or number of each word, and then she went back to the beginning and wrote down the second letter or number of each word. She kept going until all of the letters were in the grid. When she was finished, she sat back and threw her pencil down triumphantly.

"Easy!" she announced. Lili and Eli peered at her notebook.

I	F	Y	O	U	W	A	N
T	T	O	J	O	I	N	T
H	E	M	M	M	E	E	T
U	S	T	O	M	O	R	R
O	W	N	I	G	H	T	A
T	7	3	0	I	N	T	H
E	N	O	R	T	H	W	E
S	T	W	O	O	D	S	

Lili read it out loud: "'If you want to join the MM, meet us tomorrow night at seven thirty in the northwest woods.' Wow, Erin, I'm impressed. That was super-smart!"

Eli nodded in agreement as Erin blushed. "It was nothing," she said modestly.

Lili turned to Eli. "Do you know what they mean by the northwest woods?"

"I think so," Eli said. He brought up the Atkinson website on his laptop and clicked on the campus map.

"Your school sure is fancy," Erin said as she looked at the large drawing that showed six different buildings, as well as sports fields and tennis courts.

"It's big, too," Eli said. He pointed at the screen. "I'm pretty sure they are talking about this part. It's the wooded area behind the sports fields."

Lili looked worried. "Are you sure it's safe?"

"Don't worry, I'll bring a flashlight with me." Eli tried to reassure his sister, but inside he felt a little nervous, too. After all, he didn't know who the members of the Memento Mori were.

After his Computer Club meeting the next day, Eli said good night to his friends, grabbed the flashlight he had brought from home, and made his way through the dark Atkinson grounds. He started on the path that went through the woods and looped to the west.

"I hope I'm right," he mumbled to himself as the woods closed around him. He shivered nervously and ran his hand through his spiky black hair. It sure was creepy back here.

The path started to veer to the left. *I'm almost there*, he thought. The beam of the flashlight created sinister-looking shadows as he walked. He tensed and stood still as he heard a rustling noise in the woods. The sound faded, and he began to travel the path again. His nerves were starting to get the better of him. The flashlight was shaking in his hands. For just a second, the beam of light moved off the path, plunging the trail ahead of him into darkness.

Eli almost screamed when a creature jumped out of the shadows. But it wasn't a creature at all. His hands were shaking so hard that he almost dropped the flashlight. Eli was looking right into the dark hollow eyes of a grinning skeleton!

Chapter Six

Eli's feet were glued to the ground, even though his brain was yelling at him to run. He forced himself to direct the flashlight beam onto the thing in front of him.

Not one, but two skeletons stood before him, blocking his path. *Wait a minute — they're wearing hoodies, jeans, and sneakers!* Eli thought. *They're guys wearing skull masks!* He took a deep breath.

The taller of the two extended his hand toward Eli. In it was an envelope.

"Take this," he said in a deep, muffled voice. "If you accept this challenge and are successful, you will be a Memento Mori. If you fail, you will never hear from us again."

They both nodded ceremoniously at Eli before disappearing into the shadows.

Eli felt his heart pounding in his chest as he hurriedly made his way back down the path, clutching the envelope and the flashlight.

There was no way he was opening it until he was somewhere indoors with lots of light!

The next day, the Jewels called an emergency meeting with the Rivals to discuss what was in the envelope. This time, they all gathered in Lili's bedroom.

"Is it okay to talk in front of him?" Ryan jerked a thumb at Eli.

Lili smiled. "Eli knows everything, and thanks to him we've got a lead on the Memento Mori."

Ryan arched an eyebrow. "Really?"

Eli nodded. "But I'm going to need your help," he said to Ryan. He told them all about his walk through the woods and his encounter with two members of the Memento Mori.

"What's in the envelope?" Erin asked eagerly.

Eli groaned. "It's a task I have to perform. If I can pull it off, I'll be a member. If I can't, it's game over."

"It can't be that bad," Veronica said, but the look on Eli's face made her ask, "or is it?"

"You tell me," Eli said. "I have to steal a pair of Arthur Atkinson's monogrammed boxer shorts and run them up the flagpole for the entire school to see. And I have to do it before this week is over or I've failed. Oh, and I can't get caught, either."

Aaron laughed. "Yeah, dude, that's bad."

Isabel wrinkled her nose, while Jasmine and Willow shook their heads. "How are you going to do it?" Jasmine asked.

"I'm hoping Ryan can help me," Eli said, "although the note was very specific that I had to do it by myself. If they spot anyone helping me, they'll consider it a failure. But I have no idea how to get a pair of Arthur Atkinson's boxer shorts!"

Ryan grinned. "Actually, it's not as hard as you might think. My uncle comes to school early every morning to do laps in the school pool. He brings his gym bag in the locker room. And I'm pretty sure he doesn't wear his boxers while he's swimming."

Eli thought it over. "How early does he get there? I have to retrieve the shorts and run them up the flagpole before anyone else gets to the school. The flagpole is right in front of the main building. I can't have anyone see me doing it."

"He's there by five thirty a.m. So if you grab the shorts right after he gets into the pool, you should have plenty of time," Ryan said. "Only one custodian is there that early. He opens up the buildings. You'll have to time it so he doesn't see you."

Eli groaned again. "I guess I'll be getting up really early tomorrow!"

45

The next morning, Eli dragged himself out of bed while it was still dark out. He had asked his mom to drop him off. Mrs. Higashida worked in Washington, DC, as a translator and left the house early each day to beat the morning rush hour.

"The Computer Club is lucky to have someone as dedicated as you," his mom said as she dropped him off in front of the school.

Eli gave her a sleepy smile as he got out of the car. His cover for being at school so early was that he was working on the supercomputer, a big project that had been the focus of the Computer Club for the entire year. It wasn't a lie, really. He planned to do just that as soon as he successfully completed the stunt.

Eli climbed the steps of the main building and strode into the deserted school. He walked down the empty hallways and past Arthur Atkinson's office. The lights were on, but the director of Atkinson Prep was not inside, so Eli made his way to the other side of the building, which housed the locker rooms, gymnasium, and indoor pool.

He stopped outside the locker room and listened for sounds of anyone moving around inside. All was silent. Eli slowly opened the door and peeked in. The room looked empty. He noticed a suit dangling from a hanger in front of a locker. On the floor below it was a sapphire-blue duffel bag with the initials "AA" on it. Eli crept quietly toward the bag. A sudden splash from the pool area startled him, but he relaxed once he realized it must be Atkinson diving in.

Quickly, he unzipped the duffel bag and saw a pair of plaid boxer shorts sitting on top. The Memento Mori were right. Atkinson did indeed have his initials monogrammed on them! Eli pulled a pair of scissors out of his backpack. He made two holes in the waistband of the boxers so he could attach them to the flagpole. When he was finished, he stuffed the boxers into his backpack.

With the first part of his task completed, he rapidly made his way through the school back toward the main entrance. The lights in all the hallways were on, but he didn't spot anyone, not even the early-morning custodian.

A glance at his watch told him it was five forty a.m. School wouldn't start for almost two hours, but he still had to hurry before more staff members began to arrive. He raced through the main entrance and approached the flagpole. He quickly untied the rope and lowered the flag to the ground. After removing the flag, he carefully folded it and placed it in his backpack so he could leave it safely in a storage room somewhere when he was finished. He grabbed the boxers and attached them to the rope, then hastily raised the boxers up the flagpole. It was a breezy morning and they fluttered in the wind. He had to laugh to himself. It *was* a funny sight, and the "AA" on the shorts was big enough to leave no doubt about who owned them.

Just then, the door to the main entrance opened. Eli jumped behind a bush and looked up. It was the custodian. Eli watched the man's gaze go to the flagpole. *Oh no!* Eli thought. *What if he finds me here? Will he take the boxers down before the Memento Mori can see it?* His heart pounded in his chest as he tried to be as quiet as possible. Then he heard the man chuckle softly and walk back inside.

Eli let out a huge sigh. He had done it!

Later that day, the entire school was buzzing about the practical joke.

"That was too funny." Eli's friend Zane laughed at lunch. "Everyone on my bus was cracking up when we pulled up to school. I wish I knew who did it. I heard Atkinson went ballistic when he found out."

Ryan walked by his table and winked. Eli wanted to tell his friend Zane the truth, but he knew he couldn't.

By the end of the day, Eli couldn't stop yawning. He was beat from getting up so early. He groggily walked toward his locker and opened it. An envelope fell out onto the floor. Eli quickly scooped it up. The envelope had a red wax seal on it with the initials "MM." Had he succeeded? Was he now a member of the Memento Mori?

Chapter Seven

"Great job, Eli!" Lili squealed, giving her brother a big hug. "I knew I could count on you!"

The Jewels, the Rivals, and Eli had once again gathered in Lili's bedroom. Eli's envelope did indeed contain an invitation to join the Memento Mori.

"I'm in!" Eli beamed. "And I am invited to a meeting next week."

Jasmine laughed. "I wish I could have seen Atkinson's face when he realized his boxers were flapping on the flagpole!"

Ryan smiled. "I did. He was not happy."

Eli grew nervous. "I hope he never finds out it was me!"

Erin crossed her arms in front of her. "If everyone here keeps their mouth shut, no one will ever know you had anything to do with it." She glared at Isabel.

"I know how to keep a secret." Isabel pouted. "But you have a very big mouth, so maybe you should be worried about yourself."

Erin's face grew bright red. "You — you —" she stuttered.

Willow let out a piercing whistle. "Quiet!" she yelled. Isabel and Erin stopped and stared at her, their mouths hanging open. "No time for fighting. Eli has more news to share."

Eli nodded. "That's right. In addition to the envelope in my locker, the Memento Mori emailed me a secret file about the history of their group. I have twenty-four hours to study the file before a code embedded in it causes it to destroy itself. They are going to test me at the next meeting before I am formally initiated." He began typing on his laptop to pull up the file. "Here it is!" he said triumphantly.

They all gathered around the laptop excitedly. Isabel bumped into Erin. Erin turned to glare at her, but a warning look from Willow silenced them both.

Ryan bent his head over the screen and let out a low whistle. "Wow," he said. "It looks like this lists the name of every single person who was ever a member of the Memento Mori."

"Oh my gosh!" Veronica cried as she pointed at the screen. "Erika Douglas, 1985. That's my biology teacher. Her name is Douglas-Kollet now, but she went to Atkinson!"

Aaron pushed his way to the front. "I wonder if any of my teachers are on here," he said.

Ryan cleared his throat. "Excuse me, but we don't have time for this. We only have twenty-four hours before the file is deleted. Let's get to work."

Willow nodded her head. "Agreed," she said. Ryan looked at her in surprise. She shrugged. "When you're right, you're right," she told him with a grin.

Eli began to read from the file. "It has a history of the Memento Mori, too. This is interesting. Memento Mori means 'remember your mortality' in Latin. The group believes in living every day like it is their last, and celebrating life." He smiled. "I'm kind of glad you guys talked me into this. It sounds like it's a fun group to be a part of." His smile turned to an evil grin. "And I might even get used to those skull masks."

Lili rolled her eyes. "Oh no! We've created a monster!"

"I did it all for you, sis," Eli teased back. He returned his attention to the computer and continued scanning the file. "Ryan's right. It has a list of every person to ever belong to the Memento Mori since it first was formed, dated by year."

"Search 1949," Erin and Isabel said at the exact same time. They looked at each other in surprise, while the rest of the group burst out laughing.

"I guess you guys have some things in common after all," Jasmine said. Erin and Isabel rolled their eyes at this comment simultaneously, causing everyone to erupt in fresh peals of laughter.

Eli ignored the ruckus as he typed in "1949." A list of eight names popped up.

Isabel scanned the list. "They must all be old men by now. Some of them might not even be alive."

Willow read the names. " 'Henry Porter. Robert Everette. Thomas Roderick. Lawrence Andover. Walter Donahue. David Wimmer. James Kirk. Arthur Clifford.' I guess we could do an Internet search on each of them and see what we turn up."

Erin tapped a finger to her cheek, deep in thought. "One of those names sounds so familiar, but I can't place it. Willow, can you read them again?"

Willow repeated the list, while Erin shut her eyes tightly. "I know I've heard one of those names recently. It's floating around my brain. I just can't grab it!"

"Think of something completely different," Lili suggested. "That always works for me. Did you see last night's episode of *East Coast Class*? I loved the white dress Derrica wore to the party. Too bad Rhianna threw that glass of punch on her."

Erin got a huge grin on her face. "Lili, I love you!" She grabbed her surprised friend in a hug. "That's it! Derrica mentioned Lawrence Andover on her Chatter page."

East Coast Class was a reality television show about rich social-ites in the DC area. The Jewels had had a chance to meet one of the stars of the show, Derrica, when they tried to stop the Rivals from stealing her emerald. Derrica knew all about Arthur Atkinson's involvement with the theft and about how he was searching for the sapphire, too.

Eli handed his laptop over to Erin. She logged into her Chatter account and went straight to Derrica's page, then read one of her status updates out loud: "Congrats to Chad Andover and Amanda Highfield on their engagement. Looking forward to the party this Saturday night at Lawrence Andover's house!"

"Maybe Chad is Lawrence's grandson?" Aaron suggested.

"I know one way we can find out!" Erin began to type. "I'll ask Derrica."

The next day, the Rivals, the Jewels, and Eli sat at Café X again, this time to meet Derrica. She had confirmed that Lawrence was indeed her friend Chad's grandfather, and was thrilled to hear from Erin. She wanted to talk in person as soon as possible.

Veronica looked uneasy. "Is everything okay?" Erin asked as she sipped on a vanilla frappe.

"We stole her emerald," Veronica said. "I feel really bad about it."

Ryan, Aaron, and even Isabel had guilty looks on their faces.

"Derrica is really nice," Jasmine tried to reassure them. "She'll be happy you're trying to help get it back."

Just then, Derrica breezed through the door, wearing oversized sunglasses and carrying a clearly expensive handbag. She let out a little yelp of excitement when she spotted the Jewels.

"Girls!" She hurried over, her high heels clicking on the floor. "It's been ages." She bent to give them all air kisses, then removed her sunglasses and turned her gaze to the Rivals. "Are these the little masterminds who stole my lucky emerald?"

The Rivals all looked uncomfortable, but Ryan spoke first. "We did, and we're sorry," he said while the others nodded. "Once we turned the jewels over to my uncle, he locked them in the safe in his house. But we're going to do everything we can to get it back for you."

Derrica waved a perfectly manicured hand in the air. "I understand. It was all that awful Arthur Atkinson's fault. Water under the bridge. If you can get my emerald back, all will be forgiven." She looked at Erin. "So you wanted to know about Lawrence Andover?"

"Yes," Erin said. "In fact, we need a favor. We were hoping you could introduce us to him. We think he might know something about the Atkinson sapphire."

"Hmmm," Derrica pondered. "Well, it will have to be during the engagement party. He's taking a long trip to the south of France the next day."

"Do you think you can get us in?" Erin asked eagerly.

"It would be hard to sneak all of you in," Derrica admitted. "Does it have to be everyone?"

The group exchanged confused glances. They hadn't thought about splitting up. Willow took charge.

"Eli needs to go," Willow explained. "He's Lili's brother, and a member of the same secret organization at Atkinson that Lawrence was a part of. If Mr. Andover knows anything about the sapphire, we're hoping he might open up to Eli."

Ryan jumped in. "And Willow and I should be there," he said. Willow looked at him in surprise, and he smiled.

"Are you sure we should all be seen together? Isn't your uncle getting suspicious that you're hanging out with us?" Jasmine asked. "I mean, he seems to have eyes everywhere, you know?"

Ryan shook his head. "I happened to mention that we were doing some field research to get ready for Nationals, to throw him off track, so we can meet with Mr. Andover without drawing attention to ourselves, no problem. Aaron is a master of disguise, so we should bring him along, too, just in case. Also, it's probably a good idea to have a history expert."

Isabel eagerly leaned forward, but Willow insisted on taking Erin. "It should be two Jewels and two Rivals," she explained. "It's only fair."

"So what are the rest of us supposed to do?" Jasmine asked.

"Maybe you can keep researching what the treasure might be," Willow said. "We still have no clue and we don't want to waste time looking for an answer."

Jasmine nodded. It wasn't the most fun assignment, but it was still important.

"Now that that's decided," Derrica said, "I'll have to figure out how to get you in. The Andover mansion is beautiful — and huge. Our families have been friends for years, so I know the layout pretty well. Let me think it over and I'll message Erin and let her know. I've got to run now. I'm late for a fitting at Elan's," she said as she stood up.

Lili's eyes grew wide. "Oh, please post a photo of you wearing Elan's latest creation!"

Derrica laughed. "I will, darling. I'll be in touch. Ta-ta!" She floated out of the café.

Veronica shook her head in disbelief. "She is exactly the same as she is on television. And I thought all reality shows were fake!"

The following Saturday, Eli, Willow, Erin, Ryan, and Aaron met at Ryan's house, which turned out to be within walking distance of the Andover mansion. The mansion, built of red stone, was impressive, and Willow quickly counted over thirty windows in the front of the house. It had a huge front lawn and a circular driveway, complete with a fountain in the middle.

Erin read from her phone. "Derrica said to go to the French doors off the library at four p.m. Then we're supposed to walk around to the back of the house, and the library will be located to our left. Derrica will let us in and bring us to Andover for a meeting."

Guests were already driving up and valets were parking their cars for them. The team decided to walk on the far side of the lawn, which had a row of trees planted next to the driveway, so as not to draw any attention to themselves.

They rounded the house and came to the back, where they saw the gleaming glass French doors, just as Derrica had described. Eli reached his hand to the doorknob and turned it, but the door was locked.

"Did Derrica forget?" Aaron asked, panicked.

If Derrica didn't come through, they would miss their chance to talk to Mr. Andover!

A moment later, the handle of the door turned slowly. Derrica poked her head out. "Just in time!" she said in a loud whisper. "Mr. Andover is in the library."

The group exchanged excited glances. Answers to all their questions about the sapphire could be waiting for them just on the other side of that door!

Chapter Eight

They walked into a large room that still felt cozy despite its size, due to the burgundy carpet on the floor, the dark leather armchairs in front of the fireplace, and the tall mahogany bookcases that stretched from floor to ceiling and filled every inch of wall space. Sitting in one of the chairs was a thin man with a lined face and neatly combed, wavy white hair. He wore a tuxedo and had a plaid blanket on his lap.

"Lawrence, these are the students who wanted to meet you," Derrica said, motioning to them.

"Come in, come in," he said, and it was hard to read his mood. He wasn't smiling, but he didn't sound unfriendly, either. "Hope you don't mind standing. Or the fire, either, for that matter. I know it's late in the spring, but it still feels like winter in my bones."

Derrica stepped back and Willow, Erin, Eli, Ryan, and Aaron awkwardly gathered around Mr. Andover.

"It's nice to meet you, Mr. Andover," Willow said politely. "And thank you for having us."

"It's a good excuse to hide in here for a bit longer," the man replied. "These parties are so terribly boring. A nap is more exciting. But I suppose talking to you will have to do. What is it you all wanted? Derrica didn't say."

"Well, I'm Ryan Atkinson," Ryan began, carefully emphasizing his last name.

Mr. Andover's face brightened. "You're my old friend Charlie's grandson, aren't you? My goodness, I miss that old boy. So do you and your friends go to the school?"

"Yes. And Aaron and Eli do, too," Ryan said, pointing to the other boys.

"And we go to Martha Washington," Erin offered.

"A fine school," Mr. Andover said with a nod. "My, I remember the pranks we used to play on those girls. Had them convinced a ghost was haunting their dining hall! Those were the days."

The old man was smiling now, and he had a distant look in his eyes. Willow and Ryan exchanged glances. He had mentioned "pranks." They were both thinking the same thing. This might be a good time to mention the Memento Mori.

"That's what we came to see you about, sir," Ryan said. "We had some questions about one of the pranks played by the Memento Mori."

"And how do you know about that?" Mr. Andover asked, narrowing his eyes.

Eli stepped forward. "I'm a member, sir," he said. "I saw your name in the roster."

Mr. Andover nodded approvingly. "So, what did you have to do to get in?"

"Well, I had to run Arthur Atkinson's boxer shorts up a flagpole," Eli admitted, blushing a little.

To everyone's surprise, Mr. Andover let out a huge guffaw. He laughed and laughed until Derrica ran up and patted him on the back.

"Lawrence, are you all right?" she asked.

"Better than I have been in years," he replied, wiping away tears. "Oh boy, that's rich. What a classic! I wish I could have seen it. Did you take a picture?"

Eli shook his head. "I was too nervous."

Ryan tapped the screen of his phone and then held it out to Mr. Andover. "It's all over the Internet. See?"

The old man chuckled. "Couldn't have happened to a better person. Ryan, your uncle was always a mean little child. My guess is he's grown up to be a nasty man."

Ryan nodded. "You could say that," he replied, a little sadly.

Mr. Andover took a deep breath. "So. What was your question about the Memento Mori?"

Ryan looked at Eli and gave a small nod. It would be better if Eli asked, since Mr. Andover seemed to like his prank so much.

"Well, it's like this," Eli said, a little nervously. "We need to find the Atkinson sapphire. And we think that maybe the Memento Mori took it as a prank when you were in it."

Mr. Andover eyed Eli for a moment without saying anything. The quiet seemed to drag on for a long time. Finally, he began to speak softly.

"It was so long ago," Mr. Andover said. "But silence is most precious to the Memento Mori. I do not think I could betray that trust, even now."

"I know," Eli said. "But, sir, I read the handbook. Doesn't it also say that the members of the Memento Mori live by a code to do what is right? In this case, telling us about the sapphire is the right thing to do." Eli went on to explain Arthur Atkinson's scheming and how he had tricked a bunch of kids into stealing jewels for him. Mr. Andover's face grew grave as he listened to Eli's account of Arthur's actions. "So, if you tell us what you know about the sapphire, sir, you can help stop him," Eli concluded.

Mr. Andover nodded thoughtfully. "What a bright young man you are. A credit to the Memento Mori, for sure," he said. "Very well. I shall come clean, for the common good."

Eli and the others anxiously waited for him to continue. What did Mr. Andover know?

"Yes, the Memento Mori took the sapphire," he said. "As a prank, just as you have guessed. But the hubbub it caused scared us. There was even talk of bringing in the FBI! So we hid it, and vowed never to speak of it."

The kids all looked at one another, excited. Their guess was right!

"Thank you for telling us," Willow said.

Mr. Andover's voice grew sad. "My Memento Mori brothers are all gone now. I am the last. And the sapphire should be returned to the school, after all. It's only right."

"That's exactly what we plan to do," Ryan said quickly. "The sapphire belongs back at Atkinson."

"Can you tell us where it's hidden?" Willow asked eagerly.

"I wish I could," Mr. Andover said. "But Bobby's the one who hid it. We decided only one of us should know, for safety. And he's pushing up daisies now."

Willow felt like a deflated balloon. They had come so close — only to lose the trail!

"Except . . ." Mr. Andover said slowly. "I remember now. Walter said that Bobby would have to leave some kind of clue, in case anything ever happened to him, so the rest of us could figure it out."

"And do you remember what it was?" Erin asked.

Mr. Andover quickly stood up and surprised them all by moving swiftly along the bookcases.

"It's here somewhere," he said. Then he pulled out an old leather-bound notebook. "Ah, got it!"

"The clue?" Ryan asked.

"It's my journal from 1949," the old man replied. "Hmm . . . let's see. Here it is! 'The first clue is in the painting in the library.'"

"What painting?" Ryan asked.

"And what library?" followed Willow.

"Atkinson Library, I'm sure," Mr. Andover said thoughtfully. "As for the painting, I don't remember. And I didn't write it down, either. Probably why I got all those Cs in school. I was a terrible note taker. I'm sorry."

"Don't be," Erin said quickly. "This is a big help. Now we know where to start looking."

"It's my pleasure," Mr. Andover said, smiling at the young faces assembled before him. "I haven't had this much fun in a long time. If I remember anything else, I'll let Derrica know."

"Thank you so much," Willow said.

"And you tell me if you find the sapphire, will you?" Mr. Andover asked.

"Of course," Ryan promised.

"Wonderful," said Mr. Andover. "And now, before you go, I need you to do one more thing for me."

"What's that?" Eli asked.

Mr. Andover grinned. "Can you show me that picture of the flag-pole again?"

Chapter Nine

"So let me get this straight," Jasmine said. "We have to look at all of the paintings in the Atkinson Library for some clue . . . and we don't even know what it is? How many paintings are there?"

After meeting Lawrence Andover, Willow, Erin, and the others met up with the rest of the Jewels and Rivals at Pizza Paradise in Hallytown. They all sat at a large round table, sharing two pizzas and discussing what had happened.

"Dozens," Veronica answered flatly.

"That will take forever!" Isabel wailed.

"Maybe not," Lili said, and everyone looked at her. "I mean, Memento Mori is also a term to describe a style of art. You know, stuff with skulls, mostly. So maybe the clue is in a Memento Mori painting."

"That's genius!" Erin cried.

Aaron looked excited. "I bet I know where the clue is! There's this old painting in the library of a skull on a table next to a vase with a blossoming rose in it."

"It's worth checking out," Willow said.

Ryan nodded. "And at least we know where to start."

Jasmine frowned. "Won't it look suspicious if we march into the library and start examining the painting?"

Ryan grinned. "Not when you can get in anytime you want."

The next morning, Ryan opened the door to the library at Atkinson Preparatory School.

"So you have a key to every building at the school?" Willow asked. She sounded impressed.

"It's one of the perks of being an Atkinson," Ryan said. "You never know when I might need to study on a Sunday morning."

"Or look for a painting without anyone bothering you," Erin piped up.

The library was deserted, which was just perfect. Ryan flipped a switch and the overhead fluorescent lights flickered on.

Erin let out a whistle. "Man, no wonder you guys do so good at quiz bowl. This place is awesome."

The library looked like Lawrence Andover's times ten. In the center of the room was the reading area, filled with gleaming wood desks that featured brass reading lamps at each seat. Thousands of books were shelved on rows of antique wooden shelves, not the industrial metal ones found in the Martha Washington Library.

"It is," Veronica agreed. "And it's so quiet, even on a regular day."

"The painting is over by the Mystery section," Aaron said, sprinting ahead of everyone.

"How fitting," Jasmine said dryly.

Aaron led them to a painting on the wall that was just as he had described. A gray, cracked skull sat on a brown wood table. Next to it, a rose sat in a clear glass vase.

"It's always been one of my favorites," he said, looking up at it with a smile. "It's really cool, right?"

"Cool but creepy," Lili said.

"It is hideous," Isabel said with a derisive sniff. "Can we please stop admiring it and start looking for the clue?"

Ryan reached up and took the painting off the wall.

"Are you sure we can do that?" Jasmine asked.

"Nobody's watching," Ryan pointed out. "Come on, let's get a better look."

He brought the painting to one of the reading tables and turned on the light. After further inspection, Lili noted it was an oil painting. In addition to the skull, tabletop, and vase with the rose, there was a signature on the bottom right.

"It looks like the name Hall," Aaron said. "But I've never come across a painter by that name who's associated with this style."

"Then maybe the name of the painter is the clue," Willow guessed. "Maybe the clue is that the sapphire is in the hall."

"Which hall?" Isabel asked. "There are hundreds of halls here."

"It could be, like, the main hall," Erin suggested.

"Maybe, but where?" Veronica asked.

Aaron picked up the painting. "Let's see what's on the back."

He turned it over to reveal an aged piece of brown paper on the back of the frame.

"Rats," he said with a frown. "I thought there'd be a map or something."

"There *is* something," Lili said, pointing. "Look!"

In the top left corner of the paper was a tiny skull drawn in black ink.

Ryan ran his hand over the symbol. "There's something under there," he said. Then he ran to the librarian's desk and picked up a pair of scissors.

"You can't cut it up!" Jasmine said in horror.

"I'm not hurting the painting, just the paper," Ryan assured her. "Watch."

He carefully sliced open the paper underneath the skull, then reached in and pulled out a small, folded piece of paper.

"Oh my gosh, this is so exciting!" Lili squealed.

Ryan opened it up. "It's a map," he said. "It looks like the grounds of Atkinson."

"It's got to lead to the sapphire," Willow said.

Ryan nodded. "Maybe. There's a line tracing out a route, and it starts here in the library. Let's go."

They left the library and followed Ryan across the grounds to the school's main building. He opened the door and led them past the auditorium, and then made several turns into various hallways. Finally, he stopped in front of a closed door.

"That's funny," he said. "The map says this leads to the basement, but I didn't know there was an entrance to the basement here."

He opened the door to reveal a shallow, empty closet.

"See what I mean?" Ryan asked.

Aaron tapped on the back of the closet, and a hollow sound echoed back at him.

"I bet you there's a staircase behind here," he said. "It doesn't feel like a wall."

"Ooh, it's a secret entrance!" Lili said.

"Well, we can't use scissors to cut our way through," Isabel said.

"We don't have to," Erin argued. She stepped into the closet and felt around the edges of the back wall. She pulled at a corner and a large sheet of plywood came off, revealing a dark staircase beyond.

Everyone stared in amazement. Even Erin looked surprised.

"Wow, I wasn't actually sure that would work."

Willow, Aaron, and Ryan helped Erin move the sheet of wood outside the closet. Isabel nervously peered down into the darkness.

"We should not do this without a flashlight," she said.

"It's cool," Ryan said. "I have a flashlight app on my phone."

Willow grinned at him. "Me, too."

"I'll take the lead, and you can head up the rear," Ryan said, moving toward the opening in the wall.

"I can take the lead," Willow offered.

"You could, but I have the map," Ryan said with a grin, and then he headed down the staircase.

Aaron, Veronica, and Isabel followed Ryan, and then Erin took the lead for the Jewels, followed by Lili, Jasmine, and finally Willow.

Ryan's phone illuminated just a foot or two in front of him, and Willow's light bounced off Lily's shoulders, casting spooky shadows on the dusty brick walls.

"According to the map, we go straight," Ryan called back to the others. "Just keep moving and you'll be fine."

"This is ridiculous," said Isabel as she stepped off the last stair. "I am getting dust all over my . . . *Eeeeeeekkkkkkkkkk!*"

Isabel's ear-splitting shriek echoed through the basement. She rushed forward, nearly knocking over Veronica.

"Something touched my leg!" she cried. "It is probably a hairy tarantula! Or a rat!"

Lili, Erin, and Willow quickly backed up on the stairs. Aaron and Veronica stepped away from Isabel. Ryan flashed his light around Isabel's feet.

"I don't see anything," he reported.

Erin spoke up. "Oh gosh, look at that. I must have accidentally dropped my fuzzy pen. Sorry, Isabel."

She held up a novelty pen with googly eyes and furry orange hair. Isabel looked furious.

"I do not understand why we have to work with these immature girls," she said resentfully.

"Excuse me, but if it weren't for us, you wouldn't have seen the

Memento Mori list or gotten to meet Lawrence Andover, either, for that matter," Erin shot back.

"Can you two please quit it?" Willow called out. "We're, like, just a few feet away from maybe finding the sapphire. We need to focus."

"Oh, I'm focused," Erin said, glaring at Isabel.

Isabel turned her back to Erin. "I am more focused than you."

"Great," Ryan said. He took a few steps forward. "So the map ends at this brick wall."

"And then what?" Aaron asked.

"There are some numbers," Ryan replied. "27X, 15Y."

Willow quickly moved forward. "Those are coordinates, like on a graph or a grid," the Jewels' math expert said excitedly, shining her light on the wall. "See the bricks? What if each one is a point on the coordinates?"

Ryan started to nod excitedly. "So that would be fifteen bricks from the floor, and then twenty-seven bricks in from the left," he said, counting as he talked. "Twenty-five . . . twenty-six . . . twenty-seven!"

Ryan touched the brick. "It's loose!"

"Hold up!" Erin warned. "This is the part where you grab the sapphire, then say, 'So long, suckers!' and escape through some secret passage, right?"

Ryan sighed. "Wrong. I already told you guys that you can trust us."

"That's not good enough," Erin said. "Let Willow move the brick with you."

"Fine," Ryan said impatiently. "Let's just do this."

Willow and Ryan each touched the brick and began to pry it loose. It easily came off in their hands.

"There's something in there!" Willow cried.

Ryan pulled out a black pouch, opened it, and slid the contents into Willow's open palm. His light illuminated a gleaming blue jewel.

"It's the sapphire," he said breathlessly, and the other kids let out a spontaneous cheer.

"We did it!" Erin cried.

"Let's get it back to the library so we can get a closer look," Willow suggested.

"Good idea," said Isabel. "I will be happy to get out of this *base cement*, or whatever you call it."

Ryan gave Willow the pouch. "You should carry it," he said, and Willow smiled.

They went back up the stairs, replaced the fake wall, and made sure to close the closet behind them. Then they hurried back through the deserted halls, across the campus, and returned to the library. Willow took a seat at a table while the others gathered around her. She turned on a reading light and slipped the sapphire out of its pouch.

About an inch in diameter, the round stone had beautiful facets cut into its surface. It was set in what looked like a gold circle with a ring of tiny, creamy white jewels all around it.

"It's a brooch," Jasmine said. "And those are pearls."

She gently picked it up and turned it over. The back of the jewel was open, with the bar of the brooch pin going across.

"Do you see a symbol?" Ryan asked.

"I think so," Jasmine said, pointing. "Look."

"We should take a picture of it," Ryan said, holding up his phone.

"I wouldn't do that if I were you."

The sound of a familiar voice caused them all to freeze. Arthur Atkinson was standing in the library doorway, an evil grin on his face.

"Please be so kind as to step away from my sapphire," he said.

Chapter Ten

"I knew this was a setup!" Erin yelled.

Arthur Atkinson laughed. "It was, but not the kind you think," he said with a grin, his tall frame looming over them. "When my nephew here announced that he and his friends were no longer going to play my little game, I suspected he would go behind my back and try to find the sapphire. Getting you to help him was his own idea. Smart. But unfortunately, Ryan, you weren't smart enough to make sure I wasn't following you."

Ryan's cheeks flushed red and he looked down at the table. Erin realized how difficult his relationship with his uncle must be, and that made her sympathize with Ryan. But she was angrier than ever. She quickly grabbed the sapphire.

"If you think we're handing this over, you're crazy," Erin said.

"On the contrary, I am thinking quite clearly," Atkinson replied, his voice as smooth as oil. "The sapphire belongs to Atkinson Preparatory

School. I am the director of the school. If you don't turn it over to me, I will simply call the police."

"You'd better give it to him, Erin," Jasmine whispered. At one time, the police suspected that Jasmine might have stolen the Martha Washington diamond. She didn't want to go through that terrible experience again.

"Call them," Erin said, keeping her eyes locked with Arthur Atkinson's. "We'll tell them the whole story."

"You could," Arthur Atkinson said. "But then they'd have to believe you. They didn't believe you when you said the Rivals had stolen the diamond."

"Listen to him," Ryan said. "It's not worth it."

Willow turned to Erin, and her face was serious. "I hate to say it, but Ryan's right."

Erin's grip on the sapphire was so tight that her knuckles were white. She hated to give it up, but she knew she had to. Reluctantly, she loosened her grip and handed it to Aaron.

"You do it," she said. "I don't want to go near that creep."

Aaron walked over to his principal and gave him the sapphire.

"Thank you," Arthur Atkinson said with a slick grin.

"You should," Erin said. "You couldn't have done it without us."

Atkinson slipped the sapphire into his jacket pocket and left the library without another word.

"Well, that's it," Jasmine said glumly, sinking into a chair. "Game over."

"Maybe not," Lili said, and everyone turned to look at her. She put a finger to her lips and slowly held up her right hand.

"No way!" Erin whispered.

Lili had drawn the symbol from the back of the sapphire on her palm!

Chapter Eleven

"Lili, close your hand!" Willow hissed. "We don't know if Atkinson is watching us somehow even now."

"Let's get out of here, fast," Ryan agreed.

When they got outside, they looked around to make sure Arthur Atkinson was nowhere around.

"Let's go to the Hallytown Community Center," she suggested, and then explained to the Rivals, "My mom works there."

"That should be safe," Ryan said.

"The bus to Hallytown is just a few blocks away," Willow pointed out. "We can text our parents and tell them we're studying there."

Twenty minutes later, they stepped off the local bus in front of the community center. Cheerful yellow daffodils covered the front lawn. Inside, they stopped by the main office, where Willow's mom was seated behind a desk covered with photos of Willow and her brothers.

"Willow!" Mrs. Albern looked surprised to see her daughter. "But I thought you all were studying at Atkinson."

"Well . . . Ryan forgot his key," Willow said, thinking quickly. "I was wondering if we could use the meeting room, if it's open."

"Of course!" Willow's mom replied with a smile. "It's nice to see you two teams working together. That's true sportsmanship."

"Yeah, we're practically all best friends now," Erin piped up, casting a wicked glance at Isabel, who frowned.

"Well, enjoy your studying," Mrs. Albern said. "We close in a couple of hours."

Willow led them to the meeting room, and they all took seats at the round table.

"We should check for bugs before we do anything," Jasmine said.

Erin glared at the Rivals. "Oh yeah, that's right. You guys bugged us once before."

"That was my uncle's idea," Ryan said defensively.

"All the more reason to check now," Willow said, and they all looked through their bags and clothes for anything suspicious — but found nothing.

"Okay, Lili," Erin said. "Let's see that hand."

Lili opened her palm and placed it on the table where everyone could see. The symbol she had drawn was three squares of different sizes. Their corners were touching so that the three linked sides of the squares formed a triangle.

"It's the Pythagorean theorem!" Willow and Ryan burst out at the same time.

"Let me guess," Erin said. "That's a math thing, right?"

Willow nodded. "Geometry. It's, like, a diagram that explains this theory. You see these two squares here? If you add up the areas of these two, they'll equal the area of the big square."

"Wow. My brain hurts just thinking about it," Aaron quipped. "So what does that have to do with the other clues?"

"Wait a second, that's right!" Jasmine said. "We've only seen the clue on the back of the diamond. But you guys know the clues on the back of the emerald and the ruby, right?"

"We do," Veronica replied. "But they don't make any sense. We were hoping the clue on the sapphire would shed some light on the first three."

Jasmine took out the sketchbook she always carried with her and opened it up. "Whenever we found something written about the jewels, they're in the same order: ruby, diamond, emerald, sapphire. So we should lay the clues out the same way."

"Good idea," Veronica said. "The first one should be the number one-ten followed by a little circle. That was on the ruby."

"And E-fifty was on the diamond," Willow added.

"The third clue contains a letter and a number, too," Ryan added. "It's N–two hundred."

"And then we have the symbol," Jasmine said, copying it into the book. It felt strange and exciting to see all the clues together after searching for them for so long.

Willow frowned at the clues. "That doesn't seem to clear things up at all."

"So wait a second," Erin said. "You mean you guys have had the first three clues for weeks and haven't figured out anything about them yet?"

"It is not that easy," Isabel said defensively.

"But, guys, that's a good thing," Jasmine pointed out. "That means that Arthur Atkinson is as clueless as we are. And if he needed us to find the sapphire for him, then he can't be that bright. No offense, Ryan."

"It's cool," Ryan said. "Uncle Arthur is not famous for his brains in my family. Dad says they let him be the director of the school just so he doesn't mess up the family's big companies."

Erin rolled her eyes. "Nice. Stick him in charge of a bunch of kids."

"He might not be smart, but he can hire people who are," Ryan reminded them all. "So we'd better try to figure the clues out first."

"Maybe it's a mathematical formula," Willow suggested. She opened up the calculator on her phone and began typing in numbers.

"The N and E could stand for directions — north and east," Erin pointed out.

"We thought of that already," Isabel said with a sniff. "But it is no good without knowing more about the location."

"Maybe they're addresses," Lili suggested. "Have you checked addresses in the DC area that match? You know, like one hundred North Street or something like that?"

Ryan nodded. "There are lots of streets like that. It's hard to narrow it down."

"And that still doesn't explain the Pythagorean symbol at the end," Willow added.

They all sighed at once, followed by an uncomfortable silence. Then Veronica's wristwatch began to beep.

"Oh no! We've got quiz bowl practice!" she cried.

"You guys practice on a Sunday?" Erin asked.

"We practice all the time," Isabel said. "Which is why we always beat you."

"Not always," Erin shot back. The Jewels had beaten the Rivals the last time they'd gone head-to-head.

"We'll have to finish this argument some other time," Ryan said, standing up. "In the meantime, let's keep working on the clues. We can text each other if we figure out anything."

"And how do we keep your uncle from spying on us in the meantime?" Erin asked.

Ryan frowned. "I don't know. Let me check my room at home. Maybe he bugged me there. But our texts should be safe."

"My mom's going to be outside in five minutes to get us," Veronica said, looking up from her cell phone. "We'd better go."

The Rivals left, leaving the Jewels alone in the meeting room.

"You know what I'm thinking?" Willow asked.

"That we need to figure out the clues before Arthur Atkinson does?" Jasmine asked.

Willow shook her head. "No, that we need to study, too. I don't want to fall behind in quiz bowl just because we're solving the jewel-thieving mystery of the century!"

Chapter Twelve

"Achoo!" Erin's loud sneeze ricocheted through Hallytown High School's auditorium, causing several people, including Willow and Jasmine, to jump.

"Hold still!" Lili scolded behind the curtain as she once again patted Erin's face with a large cosmetics puff. Drifts of powder settled in Erin's reddish-blond hair, and she shook her head to get it off. Lili sighed. "Honestly, Erin, don't you want to be camera ready?"

After two days of marathon study sessions, the Jewels were ready to compete in a quiz bowl tournament that would be broadcast on a local cable channel. They were competing in the local high school's auditorium because of its A/V capabilities.

Erin folded her arms in front of her and stuck her tongue out at Lili. "The camera will just have to deal with my face as it is," she said.

Lili shot an exasperated look at Erin before hopefully offering up her makeup bag to Willow and Jasmine.

"No way!" Jasmine said, while Willow fiercely shook her head.

"At least we're all wearing my new and improved T-shirts!" Lili said, pointing to her top. It was the same red shirt with the words "Jewels Rule" stenciled on the front that the girls had worn the last time they had beaten the Rivals, but Lili had added brightly colored fake gems to the shirts.

"They were missing something." Lili beamed. "Now they're perfect!"

"They brought us luck last time we faced the Rivals," Jasmine added. "It will be weird competing against them today. After getting to know them and all."

Willow nodded. "I'm really surprised the Rivals even agreed to do it. It's only for fun. A win won't count toward our stats, and the Rivals only play to better their national standing."

"It's the new and improved Rivals," Erin joked in a fake commercial announcer's voice. "Now twenty-five percent softer and more likable."

The girls erupted into laughter as Ms. Keatley hurried over.

"Girls," she said in a loud whisper. "They're getting ready to start. We have to be quiet. In fact, there's a classroom we can wait in until it's our turn."

The girls followed Ms. Keatley out of the auditorium.

"The high school teams will go first," she explained once they entered the hall and walked toward a classroom door. "Then it will be you versus the Rivals, the top two middle school teams from the entire county." Ms. Keatley beamed with pride as she said this. "They are going to film all the matches today, but each one will air as its own episode."

Standing in front of the door was Mr. Haverford, the Rivals' advisor. His eyes lit up when he saw Ms. Keatley.

"Just the person I was looking for!" he said. "Do you have a second to talk about Nationals?"

"Sure." Ms. Keatley smiled at him. "Girls, go inside, find a seat, and relax."

They walked into the classroom to find Ryan, Veronica, Isabel, and Aaron, wearing their blue Atkinson uniforms. Willow hurried over to Ryan. "Did you find any bugs in your room?"

Ryan shook his head. "No. But I'm going to keep looking. My uncle has access to some pretty high-tech gear."

Aaron walked up to talk with Ryan and Willow, and the other Jewels took a seat. Erin gave a smile and wave to Veronica, who had her earbuds in. She smiled back, but it was clear that her pre–quiz bowl routine included psyching up with music, not chitchatting.

Lili held up her makeup bag again and looked at Jasmine with her big brown eyes.

"Uh-oh! She's doing puppy dog eyes," Erin warned Jasmine. "Look away! Look away!"

"How about just a smidge of lip gloss?" Lili pleaded.

Jasmine sighed as she gave in. "Fine."

"There is no resisting Lili when she does that," Erin said as Lili eagerly dug through her bag.

Erin riffled through her own backpack and pulled out some Martha Washington books that she had checked out from the school library weeks ago. She flipped through them one more time, hoping to find something — anything — that might shed light on the clues that were etched into the gems. As she began to read, she felt someone sit down in the seat next to her. She looked up from her book — it was Isabel!

"I've been meaning to get this one," Isabel said, her green eyes devouring the cover eagerly. "May I see it?"

"Sure," Erin said in surprise. She still felt on guard when it came to Isabel, but she handed the book over.

Isabel studied it carefully. "I love how Martha is portrayed as young and beautiful here. So many people know her only as a frumpy old lady."

"If you like this book, you should see the others I have." Erin couldn't help sharing. She loved history and loved to talk to other history enthusiasts, although she never in a million years thought she'd be talking with Isabel like this. She reached into her backpack and pulled out some of the older and rarer books about Martha. "Our library has an amazing collection of books about her."

Isabel pulled a folder from her own backpack and took from it a photocopy of an old letter. "This is a letter written from George Washington to Martha. It's one of only five letters between them that survived. Martha burned all of their correspondence after George's death."

Erin nodded. "She wanted to keep things private. Who could blame her? They were the equivalent of movie stars back then. Everyone wanted to know all their personal business. When I found an original letter she wrote, I was so totally excited!"

Isabel's eyes grew wide. "An original letter?"

Erin found herself telling Isabel the story of how the Jewels discovered a letter from Martha to a person they thought might be Abigail Adams — and how Martha described the four jewels.

"That's what first made us realize the ruby was part of something bigger," Erin explained, despite it feeling really weird to talk to Isabel like this. "Then we found Martha's diary, and that's what led us to the Townsend desk at the Met and the diamond."

Isabel clasped her hands and stared into space, looking thoughtful. "You know, we have a letter, too. But it's not from Martha Washington. It's *to* her."

"Do you have it with you?" Erin asked excitedly.

Isabel reached into her bag again. "Yes, I have a copy on my tablet." But before she could pull it out, Ms. Keatley stuck her head in the room. "It's showtime, girls! Are you ready?"

The Jewels and the Rivals stood up at the same time. Ryan looked at Willow and gave her an awkward grin, not his usual smug smile. Willow felt a momentary feeling of surprise, but she understood how he was feeling. This would be the first time they'd be competing as friends and not enemies — but only one team could win.

Chapter Thirteen

"This match goes to the Atkinson Prep Rivals!" announced the quiz bowl moderator.

The audience applauded. The Rivals high-fived, while the Jewels huddled together on the side of the stage. It was hard not to be disappointed. Nationals was only weeks away, and losing to the Rivals now seemed like a bad omen — and a step backward.

"We may have lost, but we played great," Willow consoled them. Normally she hated losing, but it had been a close contest, and they had performed well. "The match had to go into a tiebreaker and everything. We lost by only one question."

They shook hands with the Rivals and rushed off the stage. For the first time ever, the Rivals didn't smirk or tease them. In fact, they only had one thing on their minds.

"We need to get together and figure out our next move," Aaron whispered to Jasmine as they left the stage.

"Agreed," Jasmine said. Erin overheard them and jumped in. "Isabel needs to show me something. It could be important."

When they got offstage, they found Principal Frederickson waiting to be the first to greet them. As usual, she was dressed smartly: this time in a navy-blue suit jacket and matching skirt with a crisp white blouse.

"You performed magnificently," she said. "Such a credit to our school."

Willow beamed with pride. "Thanks," she said.

"I can tell that you've been concentrating on your studies . . . and not on other things," the principal said, giving them a stern look.

Jasmine cast a nervous glance at Willow. Did Principal Frederickson know that they were still searching for the treasure?

Luckily, Ms. Keatley walked up, and Principal Frederickson politely stepped aside. "Great job, girls," she said as she hugged them. "You have a shot at the Nationals, that's for sure!"

Erin agreed, "You're right, Ms. Keatley, but I'm still bummed. Why don't we invite the Rivals out for pizza to cheer us up?"

Ms. Keatley raised her eyebrows. "Really?" she asked as she looked at each girl. They all smiled and nodded.

"I already made arrangements with your parents to take you out for pizza after the match. I'm just surprised you want the Rivals to come along with us, but if that's what you want," she said, "then I'll ask Josh — I mean, Mr. Haverford."

They crowded into Ms. Keatley's VW Bug and followed Mr. Haverford, who drove the Rivals to Pizza Paradise. It was only a few minutes away from the high school, and soon they were all inside, breathing in the aroma of freshly baked pizza.

"Yum!" Lili said as she sniffed the air.

"Double yum!" Erin cried. "Competing at quiz bowl always makes me hungry."

After ordering, they began to look for somewhere to sit. There was a table for eight in the back of the room.

"Ms. Keatley, may we sit here?" Willow asked. "This is the biggest table."

Ms. Keatley nodded. "Sure, Mr. Haverford and I will sit at this table next to you." She pointed to a two-person booth. Mr. Haverford smiled at Ms. Keatley, and Ms. Keatley blushed.

Jasmine exchanged amused glances with Aaron. Both the Rivals and the Jewels had noticed Mr. Haverford had a huge crush on Ms. Keatley for a while now. She had been completely oblivious, but it looked like she finally might be figuring it out. Ryan laughed as he sat down.

"If they get married and have a family, they can start their own toddler quiz bowl team," Erin joked. "They'll be hard to beat!"

"Maybe for you," Isabel sniffed. Erin felt her cheeks flush, but Isabel quickly apologized. "I'm sorry," she gave a genuine smile. "It's just a bad reflex. You guys almost beat us, I'll admit it."

Veronica, happy over her team's win, wasn't about to count out the Jewels, either. "It was a close match. We're going to have to study extra hard for Nationals if we want to beat you!"

They dug into slices of hot, cheesy pizza, munching away as they talked. Ms. Keatley and Mr. Haverford were deep in conversation at the next table, so the two teams could speak freely.

Isabel began to fill them in on the letter as she got her tablet out. "It's from a Samuel Lindley to Martha Washington. He was a silversmith and he definitely helped her with something. But we haven't been able to get anything useful out of it."

The Jewels exchanged excited glances before Erin spoke up. "Martha mentioned a 'trustworthy jeweler' in her letter to Abigail. Silversmiths and jewelers were the same thing back then, right? Maybe it's the same jeweler?"

Isabel shrugged. "I'll read it to you. Maybe you can find something in it that we missed." She tapped the screen on her tablet and began to read aloud:

94

" 'To Mrs. Martha Washington

Dear Madam:

It gives me particular pleasure to hear that both you and General Washington are in good health. I am exceedingly obliged to you for your trust in me and promise the items have been set and are well dispersed.

Moreover, I want to assure you of my dedication to the peace and liberty for which we have so long contended. Over time our cause will be victorious. Understandably the strain of war leaves much sorrow. Now is the time to remain ever hopeful. The tumultuous days ahead cannot be avoided, but know I have done everything possible to aid you. Virginia has no British troops upon its soil at this time. Everything points to triumph. Report back when you are able, as I am most eager to hear any news. Night is falling and I bid you good evening. Our only course is to bear our burdens patiently. Never forget that I am your dutiful servant, always.

With great esteem,
Samuel Lindley
Silversmith' "

Jasmine gasped. "It must be the same jeweler from Martha's letter! Remember, she asked the jeweler to set the ruby, diamond, emerald, and sapphire for her. I think Lindley not only set them, but made sure they were separated. Maybe that's what he meant by 'well dispersed.' Martha didn't want all the jewels found together, remember?"

Aaron slumped in his chair. "But there's no hint about where the treasure is hidden," he groaned. "We're no better off than we were before."

"If the treasure was hidden, why didn't he or somebody else get it after the war?" Willow asked. "Or maybe someone did and all this is for nothing."

Isabel shook her head, her short blond hair swinging around her face. "I have done some research on Samuel Lindley. He died in 1780, three years before the war ended."

Veronica leaned forward on the table, her eyes gleaming. "Maybe he took the secret of where the treasure was hidden to the grave with him. It could still be hidden away after all these years."

Ryan nodded. "It's a possibility. But where is it hidden?"

Lili snapped her fingers. "What if there is a code in the note, kind of like a hidden message or something? Like the Memento Mori sent to Eli. Lindley would have wanted Martha to know where the treasure was, right?"

Isabel and Erin both spoke at the same time: "I love codes!" They looked at each other in surprise and everyone burst out laughing.

"Maybe they are long-lost sisters," Aaron joked.

Isabel handed over her tablet to Erin, who grabbed a notebook out of her backpack. "It helps if I write it out line by line. Makes you pay attention to each and every letter."

She began to write as Isabel leaned over her shoulder, watching every letter carefully. "It could be an acrostic puzzle," Isabel suggested eagerly.

Erin continued to write, her lips pursed in concentration. "Maybe, but if so, it's not hidden in the first paragraph."

"What's an acrostic puzzle?" Veronica wondered as the girls worked.

"It's when a recurring feature in the written words spells out a word or message," Aaron, the Rivals' arts and literature expert, explained. "Like the first word of every sentence or paragraph."

Lili nodded in agreement. "It's a form of poetry, too."

Erin dropped her pen and looked at Isabel, who was grinning from ear to ear. "We did it! We did it!" Erin shouted.

Ms. Keatley and Mr. Haverford looked over at them, startled. "What did you do, Erin?" Mr. Haverford asked.

"Um, we ate all the pizza," Erin said quickly. "I'm a lifetime member of the clean plate club so that makes me happy."

The teachers laughed and returned to their conversation.

"What did you find?" Willow asked impatiently.

"The first letter of every sentence in the second paragraph spells out the name of a place," Isabel shared, as Erin held up her notebook.

> *Moreover, I want to assure you of my dedication to the peace and liberty we have so long contended. Over time our cause will be victorious. Understandably the strain of war leaves much sorrow. Now is the time to remain ever hopeful. The tumultuous days ahead cannot be avoided, but know I have done everything possible to aid you. Virginia has no British troops upon its soil at this time. Everything points to triumph. Report back when you are able, as I am most eager to hear any news. Night is falling and I bid you good evening. Our only course is to bear our burdens patiently. Never forget that I am your dutiful servant, always.*

They all leaned over to read it. Jasmine gasped with excitement.

"The treasure is hidden at Mount Vernon!" she cried.

Chapter Fourteen

"Shhh," Willow warned. "What if Arthur Atkinson is listening?"

"I don't blame her. This is amazing," Aaron said. "I mean, it's right there in the letter. Mount Vernon, the famous home of George and Martha Washington."

Excited, Erin bolted out of her chair, knocking it over. "Let's go!" she cried.

Ms. Keatley looked up and frowned. "We're not done eating yet, Erin."

"Oh yeah, right. Sorry!" Erin tried to keep her legs from running out the door. "I'll just sit and wait." She righted her chair and sat back down in it, tapping her feet impatiently.

"Smooth move," Ryan leaned over and whispered.

Lili stuck up for her friend. "But this is big news!"

Erin's feet ricocheted along the floor. "Mount Vernon is not too far from here. We could be there in under an hour!"

"It's nighttime, Erin. Mount Vernon is closed to visitors now," Willow reminded her. "But you're right. We should go and investigate ASAP."

Erin let out a big exhalation of air. Her feet stopped tapping. "Okay. But how do we get there?"

Ryan and Willow exchanged grins, both thinking the same thing. "No problem!" Ryan said. He walked over to the booth Ms. Keatley and Mr. Haverford were sitting in, Willow right behind him.

"We had an idea," Ryan said, smiling. "We were all just talking about how field trips are a great way to study."

"Immersion learning!" Willow chimed in. "It's been working really well for us."

"Learning from experience is highly effective," Ms. Keatley said while Mr. Haverford nodded in agreement.

"To prepare for Nationals, we'd all like to visit Mount Vernon together," Ryan said. "Could we take a field trip?"

"That's a wonderful idea." Mr. Haverford beamed. He looked hopefully at Ms. Keatley. "What do you think? We could take the Atkinson Prep van and all ride down together."

"How about this weekend?" Ms. Keatley replied.

Mr. Haverford opened the calendar on his smartphone. "Does Saturday work for you?"

Ms. Keatley nodded. "It's a date!" she said. As soon as she realized what she had said, her cheeks began to turn red. "I mean, it's a date for us to take our students there, of course."

Mr. Haverford smiled at her. "Of course," he said.

"Yuck!" Ryan whispered in Willow's ear and she giggled.

"I'll be in touch with your parents to get permission slips signed," Ms. Keatley said.

Willow and Ryan returned to their chairs and waited until Ms. Keatley and Mr. Haverford were deep in conversation again before speaking.

"Today is Wednesday," Willow said. "That gives us a couple of days to try to work out the clues from the ruby, diamond, emerald, and sapphire. If we can figure that out, we'll know what to look for when we get to Mount Vernon."

Ryan frowned. "I just thought of something. My uncle's computer calendar gets automatically updated with all field trips. If he sees we're all going to Mount Vernon together, he'll be suspicious. What should we do?"

"Maybe Eli could use his computer wizardry and wipe it off the calendar?" Lili suggested.

"Does he know how to do something like that?" Ryan asked.

"Eli can do anything," Lili said confidently.

"Okay, talk to Eli and let us know what he says," Willow told Lili. "Everyone else, keep researching. If you find anything out, text us."

The next afternoon, Willow sat at her desk in her bedroom, her door shut to keep out her three little brothers. She was trying to study for the quiz bowl Nationals, but her mind kept wandering back to Mount Vernon and the clues etched on the gems. What could they mean?

She let out a big sigh before turning the volume up on the online radio station she was streaming. A little background music always helped her to concentrate. She hummed along as she read the sample math questions Ms. Keatley had given her. Willow was surprised at how much she was beginning to like the Rivals, especially Ryan. But no matter how good friends they might become, she still wanted to beat them at Nationals, and the competition was only a few weeks away. She had to focus!

She managed to work her way through a couple of sample questions before her eyes fell on the map of Mount Vernon Estate she had spread out earlier on her desk. *Hmmm*, she thought, *the main part of the estate is sort of a circle shape*. Her eyes went back to her paper and the next sample question, this one about geometry. She stared at the circle on the page. Circles. It made her think of the first clue etched on the ruby: 110°. If the little circle was a degree mark, it could refer to a point on a circle, like one hundred and ten degrees.

She sat up straight and shut the radio off. *I think I'm on to something*, she thought. She pushed the study papers aside and pulled the map directly in front of her. *If you assume that zero degrees is at the very top center of the map, then one hundred and ten degrees would be* — she ran her finger down the map — *right here!* Her finger had stopped at a point in Mount Vernon Estate right by the path leading to the fruit garden.

She tapped the map excitedly. If they started at this spot, the other clues might lead to the exact location of the treasure. Maybe, just *maybe*, she could be right! Willow grabbed her phone.

I think I've got it, she texted to all of her friends — even the Rivals. *I know where we should look when we get 2 MV!*

Chapter Fifteen

The next day after school Willow met with Ryan at Café X to talk about her discovery. She spread the map of Mount Vernon out on the table and showed Ryan how she came to her conclusion.

"So if the small circle after one hundred and ten is a degree mark, it would put us right here." She pointed to the path leading to the fruit garden.

Ryan let out a low whistle and sat back in his chair. "Wow. I never would have thought of that. I'm impressed, Willow."

Willow smiled proudly. "It's not for sure. We'll have to figure out what the E-fifty and N–two hundred mean. And then there's that Pythagorean symbol on the sapphire."

"The E and N could stand for east and north," Ryan suggested. "So maybe you need to walk that number of feet or paces in either direction."

Willow smacked a palm to her forehead. "Duh! Why didn't I think of that?"

"If you hadn't thought of the degrees, I never would have gotten that idea," Ryan said. "We're a good team. That's why I wanted your help."

They both grinned at each other for a moment before Willow said, "I talked to Lili. Eli said he couldn't delete the field trip from Atkinson's calendar, but he could move it to a different date. He's going to put it to next Saturday, not this one."

Ryan frowned. "I hope that throws him off the trail, at least for a little while. Even so, we'll have to be careful and keep an eye out for him."

Willow took out her phone and started texting. "I'm going to send a group message out to everyone to let them know what we've figured out so far. Too bad no one else could make it. Jasmine has a dance class, Lili is at an art club meeting, and Erin was forced into going to her sister Mary Ellen's ice-skating competition."

"It's hard to remember sometimes, but we do have actual lives outside all of this jewels drama." Ryan sighed. "I guess life will get back to normal once we find the treasure."

But he didn't look happy about it, and neither did Willow. They both laughed out loud after noticing each other's sad faces.

"It has been fun," Willow admitted.

"And exciting!" Ryan added.

Willow's phone beeped when she received a text message. "It's from Erin," she explained to Ryan. "She said she has a lead on the clue on the sapphire. She'll tell us on the trip to Mount Vernon. "

"Every last bit of information helps," Ryan said solemnly. "We have to do anything we can to find the treasure before my uncle does!"

Saturday morning dawned sunny and bright, with only a few fluffy white clouds dotting the sky. The Jewels and Ms. Keatley stood in front of Martha Washington School, waiting for the Rivals to pick them up.

"Today's the big day," Lili whispered to the others so Ms. Keatley wouldn't overhear her. "I wonder what we'll find!"

Jasmine bit her lip. "I don't want to get my hopes up, but I have such a good feeling. It's like I can just tell something is out there, waiting for us to find it."

"No matter what, we'll know we tried our best," Willow whispered back to her friends.

Erin nodded. "If the Jewels can't do it, no one can!"

A shiny white van with blue lettering that read "Atkinson Preparatory School" pulled into the driveway. Mr. Haverford parked the car and hopped out, walking toward Ms. Keatley with a big smile on his face.

"Your chariot awaits," he said with a bow. The girls stifled giggles as Ms. Keatley got into the front passenger seat. Mr. Haverford slid the large van doors open for them and the girls climbed inside. Isabel, Veronica, and Aaron sat in the rear row. Ryan sat in the middle and scooted over to make room for Willow and Jasmine, while Erin and Lili took the front row.

After buckling up, Erin leaned over her seat and spoke in a low voice to the others.

"I can't believe it took me this long to figure it out," Erin said. "The symbol on the sapphire — the Pythagorean theorem — it's a symbol the Masons use!"

"Of course!" Isabel added. "And George Washington was a Mason."

"What's a Mason?" Veronica wondered.

"It's the name for someone who is a member of the Freemasons, a fraternal organization for men, first formed in the sixteenth century. It still exists today," Isabel explained. "There's lots of mystery surrounding the early Masons, including hidden symbols on everything from the dollar bill to the Capitol building."

Aaron frowned. "That's interesting and all, but how does it help us understand the clues?"

Ryan shook his head. "It doesn't, but maybe it will mean something when we get to Mount Vernon."

Jasmine rubbed the side of her nose nervously, while Veronica twisted anxiously in her seat. After what seemed like forever, the van pulled into a parking lot at Mount Vernon. The Rivals and the Jewels exchanged excited glances. It was time to find out if they had guessed right.

Ms. Keatley's eyes gleamed as they walked to the main entrance. "We're in for a treat!" she said. "Dozens of the original buildings used in the Washingtons' time still stand today. It's truly like stepping back in history!"

Their first stop was the orientation center, where they watched an exciting movie about George Washington. It was hard to concentrate, though, knowing what lay ahead. Erin drummed her fingers impatiently on the arm of her chair. "Did you and Isabel figure out how to distract them?" Willow leaned over and whispered to her, nodding at Ms. Keatley and Mr. Haverford.

Erin gave a huge grin before answering. "No problemo. We got a great idea on how to do it from the Martha Washington book we were looking at the other day."

They left the visitor's center and joined the crowds of tourists walking down the pathway, admiring the green lawns and early spring flowers. Willow sprang into action.

"Since the weather is so warm today, can we start in the fruit gardens and work our way back?" Willow asked Ms. Keatley.

Their advisor shrugged her shoulders and looked at Mr. Haverford. "That's fine with me. In fact, it's a good plan. We'll beat the crowds that way, because it looks like most everyone else is heading toward the upper gardens first. Is that okay with you?" she asked Mr. Haverford.

He grinned at Willow. "Excellent suggestion."

They started out on the path that looped around the estate, heading toward the fruit gardens. When they reached the middle of the path, they had a perfect view of the Mount Vernon mansion across the large lawn. It was an impressive white brick house with a red roof and majestic columns.

"Beautiful," Lili said, her eyes wide as she took in the structure. She felt like sitting on the grass and sketching the mansion, but knew they were there on a mission. She sighed. Maybe another time.

Ms. Keatley and Mr. Haverford walked slowly behind the kids. They were deep in conversation and Ryan gave Willow a wink. This would make putting their plan into action a lot easier!

They passed the paddock that housed sheep, horses, and — a little farther up — pigs. Lili sniffed the air. "It smells like Eli's gym socks." She pinched her nose.

Willow had the map open in her hands when she stopped suddenly. "We're close," she whispered. Ryan nodded at Erin and Isabel. It was time for them to distract Ms. Keatley and Mr. Haverford while the others went in search of the treasure.

"Marie Antoinette was way more beautiful than Martha Washington!" Isabel whirled toward Erin, shouting. "Martha was an old frump!"

Erin snorted. "And you call yourself a history expert? Everyone knows now that Martha was not only a shrewd estate manager, but really pretty. Marie Antoinette may have been cute, but she wasn't that bright."

"Ha!" Isabel yelled. "Of course you're going to side with the American. What you know about French history I can fit in my little finger." She jabbed her pinky menacingly into Erin's face.

The two carried on as Mr. Haverford and Ms. Keatley rushed over. He looked at Ms. Keatley and shook his head. "Arguments over history? I didn't know that refereeing them was part of our job description."

It was the perfect distraction. While the two advisors tried to calm Erin and Isabel's fake feud, Willow ran toward the edge of the fruit garden that matched the hundred and ten degree point on the map. Jasmine, Lili, and the rest of the Rivals quickly followed behind her.

If they were right, the treasure was only two hundred fifty paces away!

Chapter Sixteen

Erin and Isabel could still be heard shouting in the distance when Willow skidded to a halt. "This is the spot that's equal to one hundred ten degrees on the estate map," she said, panting slightly.

"Two hundred paces north!" Ryan said at the exact moment Jasmine said "Fifty paces east!" They exchanged confused glances.

"We've got to go east first, then north," Jasmine quickly explained. "In all the references to the jewels we've ever found in letters or diaries they are listed in the same order: ruby, diamond, emerald, and sapphire. So if one hundred ten degrees from the ruby is the first clue, then the E-fifty from the diamond has to be the second," she insisted.

"Smart thinking," Ryan agreed.

Veronica nodded. "We can always come back and try it the other way if it's a dead end."

Willow took the lead and began to measure steady, even paces with her feet, which took them on the path that led into the fruit garden.

"Is this where George Washington chopped down the cherry tree?" Aaron joked as he eyed the fruit trees growing next to the path. Veronica shushed him. Willow was still counting.

"Forty-eight, forty-nine, fifty!" Willow stopped.

They stood at an intersection of the path, which now branched off in four different directions.

"North is left, Willow," Jasmine said. "Turn to the left and count out two hundred more steps. We're right behind you."

Willow turned and began her slow, steady counting as the others trailed behind. Jasmine felt her stomach flutter. They might be about to make the greatest discovery of their lives! Lili saw the look on her face and grabbed Jasmine's hand, giving it a little squeeze. They smiled at one another. This was it!

As Willow counted higher, they saw the path was leading them directly to a small red brick building with an old metal door.

"Gothic chic," Jasmine whispered to Lili, who smiled right back at her.

"One ninety-eight, one ninety-nine, two hundred!" Willow said triumphantly. She stood only a foot away from the front wall of the tiny structure.

"Is the treasure going to appear out of thin air now?" Aaron wondered, jokingly.

Willow consulted her visitor's guide. "It's called the Old Tomb. Washington wanted to be buried at Mount Vernon, but this tomb was deteriorating so he asked for a new one to be built. His body was moved to the new tomb after 1831, along with the remains of Martha and his other family members." Willow glanced up at the aged and weathered building. "So George and Martha were buried here before being moved to the new tomb, which I guess is why they call it the Old Tomb."

"That leaves us with the last clue from the sapphire," Lili said. "The Pythagorean or Masonic symbol, whatever you want to call it." She held up her hand. On it she had once again drawn the image found on the sapphire: three squares of different sizes, their corners touching so that the three linked sides of the squares formed a triangle. She shivered as she looked at the old building. "Will we have to go inside?"

Ryan shrugged. "Maybe. We'll have to figure out the final clue first."

Willow turned so that she was once again facing the red brick front of the Old Tomb. "Let's look around."

They all fanned out across the small front wall, looking intently at every nook and cranny in the brick surface.

"Nothing here." Ryan shook his head.

Aaron studied the old metal door with its rusty hinges. He threw his hands in the air. "Nothing on the door."

Veronica peered closer at a brick that was at about shoulder level. She squinted closely at it. "Guys! I think I found something!"

They hurriedly gathered around to peek over her shoulder. The brick she was staring at had a small, faded design carved into the upper right corner. It was the same symbol as on the sapphire!

Lili squealed and Jasmine felt her heart skip a beat.

Ryan reached out and gently touched the brick. It moved in the wall.

"It's loose!" Willow said. She looked around to make sure no other visitors were nearby. "Ryan, try and take it out."

Jasmine looked around nervously. "Some of us should shield him, in case somebody comes along."

Lili and Veronica quickly flanked Jasmine, blocking Ryan from anyone who might come down the path.

Ryan carefully pried the brick from the wall. It slid easily into his hands and he placed it on the ground. Willow and Aaron crowded around to peer into the hole. Willow used the flashlight app on her phone to illuminate the dark space. Another, older brick sat recessed in the wall. As the light beam travelled along it, they saw it had the same Masonic symbol as the outer brick had.

"Wow! I feel like I'm in a movie or something," Aaron said breathlessly.

Ryan grabbed the second brick and pulled it. Pieces broke off and crumbled as it came sliding out of the wall. He laid the second brick on the ground next to the first.

Willow aimed the light back into the hole. A mysterious bundle, wrapped carefully in decaying fabric, sat inside.

"I think we found it!" Willow cried.

Jasmine turned around to look. "What is it?"

"I'm not sure," Willow replied.

Willow and Ryan both started to reach their hands in at the same time.

Ryan quickly pulled his away. "Go for it, Willow," he said with a smile.

Willow reached inside and very gingerly pulled out the bundle. In the light of day, they could see the aged yellow fabric surrounding whatever was hidden inside. Overwhelmed by curiosity, Lili, Jasmine, and Veronica gathered around to look.

"Whatever it is, it's old," Veronica remarked.

Willow cautiously began to unwrap the fabric, some of it crumbling to dust in her hand when she touched it. As the fabric fell away, the rays of sun began to play on the item hidden inside, making it sparkle and glow.

The last piece of fabric fell off. They all gasped as they looked at the treasure cradled in Willow's hands. The smooth stone, the size of a golf ball, was like nothing Willow had ever seen before. It looked like it contained a glittering galaxy of swirling comets and stars in deep, beautiful colors: blue, red, purple, and green.

"Oh my gosh, it's a black opal!" Jasmine said excitedly. "I've never seen or heard of one this big."

"We did it!" Willow cried.

"Yes!" Ryan echoed.

Lili began jumping up and down in pure joy. Veronica beamed and grabbed Aaron in a huge hug. Everyone started laughing and cheering. They had found the treasure!

Aaron looked at the magnificent black opal, which seemed the opposite of its name as it dazzled in the sunlight. "Dude," he said to Ryan. "No wonder your uncle wanted this. It must be worth a fortune!"

A dark shadow descended over them, blocking out the sunlight.

"It is," Arthur said with an evil smile. "Hand it over."

Chapter Seventeen

Willow quickly put her hands behind her back.

"No," she said firmly. "This isn't Atkinson Prep. You're not the boss here."

Atkinson laughed. "You all seem to forget that you are children. Clever children, maybe, but still children."

"We're smarter than you," Ryan said angrily. "You wouldn't have anything if it weren't for us!"

"Again, you forget yourselves. I am the one who set you on this path to begin with," Atkinson smoothly argued. "I have known of the treasure for years . . . years! When I learned of the four jewels, I knew they must lead to something valuable beyond measure. And it looks as though I was right."

"This doesn't belong to any of us," Jasmine boldly argued. "It belongs to the Washingtons."

"You know what they say: finders, keepers . . ." Atkinson said, taking a step closer. "And I'm afraid I can't wait much longer. The salary of a school director is laughable, I'm afraid, and since my family insists on excluding me from the more profitable businesses, I must find additional streams of income."

"So you chose stealing? Nice," Jasmine said.

"It will be nice indeed, when I can stop babysitting a school full of snot-nosed brats and retire to the tropics," he said. "A black opal this size, and with this historical significance, could be worth millions."

"Too bad it's not yours," Ryan told him.

"That can easily be arranged," he said, charging toward Willow. "Give it to me!"

He was inches from Willow when she grinned and held up her hands — both empty. A look of anger and confusion crossed Atkinson's face. From the corner of his eye he saw Ryan sprinting away. Realizing that Willow must have handed the opal to him, he quickly lunged after his nephew, tackling him to the ground. Ryan pushed his uncle off and started to run again, but Atkinson grabbed his ankle, holding him down.

"Arthur Atkinson, you will stand down!"

Startled, Atkinson looked up toward the sound of the powerful female voice. A middle-aged woman marched up to him and pulled him off Ryan.

"Principal Frederickson!" Jasmine cried.

"Stay out of this!" Atkinson barked at the principal. "The boy has my treasure."

Ryan jumped up and brushed the dirt from his pants. Then he grinned and turned out his empty jeans pockets.

"Treasure? What treasure?" he asked.

Erin and Isabel came running up next, followed by Ms. Keatley and Mr. Haverford — and two burly security guards.

"Is everything all right here?" one of the guards asked.

"This man just attacked this young boy," Principal Frederickson said. "He needs to be escorted from the grounds, if not arrested."

"That is ridiculous!" Arthur Atkinson fumed. "That is my nephew, and he stole my treasure."

"I told you, I don't have any treasure," Ryan said. "Honestly, I don't know what he's talking about."

"You guys found the treasure?" Erin blurted out.

"What's all this about a treasure?" Ms. Keatley asked.

Principal Frederickson looked at Willow. "Is it true? Did you really find it?"

Jasmine stepped forward and held out her hand. The black opal glittered in the sunlight.

"It's true," she said.

Chapter Eighteen

"I'm very glad I decided to check up on you girls," Principal Frederickson said. "Things could have become very unfortunate for everyone."

A large group of people was gathered in the Martha Washington School library, where everything had started — the Jewels, Eli, the Rivals, Principal Frederickson, Ms. Keatley, Mr. Haverford, and the new acting director of Atkinson Preparatory School, Ryan's dad. After the chaotic events of the day before, they had agreed to meet and finally sort things out.

"I still don't understand," Erin said. "How did you show up at Mount Vernon at exactly the right time?"

"I never got over the feeling that you girls were still searching for the final jewel, and the treasure," she replied. "If I were your age, I would certainly find it hard to resist. Then when I saw your field trip scheduled, I thought you might be looking for clues again. I decided to go to Mount Vernon myself, and when I pulled into the parking lot, I saw Arthur Atkinson charging into the orientation center. By the time I caught up to him, he was assaulting poor Ryan."

"He didn't hurt me," Ryan said. "Anyway, I knew by running away I would distract him from whoever Willow had really given the treasure to."

"That was really smart," Willow said admiringly.

Principal Frederickson turned to Ms. Keatley. "And I would like to know why you and Mr. Haverford were not with the students."

Ms. Keatley looked a little uncomfortable. "Erin and Isabel got into a heated argument, and we tried to break it up. By the time we realized the others were gone we had lost them."

"Sorry about that," Erin said, a little sheepishly. "We knew we'd need something good to distract you with, and Isabel and I had gotten pretty good at arguing."

"Even though you always lose," Isabel said with a grin, and Erin smiled back.

"But remember, they found us again," Lili said. "All because of my awesome big brother."

Eli shrugged. "I never trusted Arthur Atkinson, so I got some of my Memento Mori friends to help me put a GPS on him. When I saw he was headed for Mount Vernon, I texted all the Jewels."

"As soon as I saw the text, I told Ms. Keatley and Mr. Haverford that the other kids were in trouble," Erin said. "Eli helped us find them because he'd pinpointed Atkinson's location. We grabbed the security guards on the way."

Ms. Keatley chimed in next. "So the whole time we've been 'immersion learning' you've really been looking for clues to a treasure?" She sounded a little hurt.

"Well, yes, but we learned a lot of stuff along the way, too," Erin said. "It helped us do better in quiz bowl, honest."

"It's still amazing to me that you guys actually found the treasure," said Mr. Haverford, holding up the Sunday newspaper. "You're famous!"

SIXTH GRADERS FIND LOST WASHINGTON TREASURE ON VERNON ESTATE, read the headline, with a picture of the black opal underneath.

Erin grinned. "Yeah, I'm glad those guards didn't believe Atkinson's story that the treasure was his."

"And I'm glad they bought *our* story that we saw that the brick was loose and the treasure dropped into our hands," Ryan added.

"I still can't believe we found such a huge black opal," Jasmine said. "No wonder Martha was keeping it hidden. They probably could have financed a whole army with it back then."

"Maybe, but I've been doing some research," Erin said. "There are some cool legends about black opals. One is that they mean bad luck for monarchs — like, for example, King George III of England. He was king during the Revolutionary War."

Veronica nodded. "I get it. So maybe it was, like, some kind of good luck charm for the Americans or something."

"Maybe we'll never know why they went to all that trouble to hide it," Lili said with a dreamy look in her eyes. "Maybe the real motive will always be a mystery."

"Whatever the reason, I'm so glad the opal will stay in Mount Vernon, where it belongs," said Jasmine. She gazed over at the empty case that once held the Martha Washington ruby. "It's too bad we don't know what Arthur Atkinson did with the other four jewels, though."

"But we do," said Ryan's dad, Charles Atkinson, a blonder and more distinguished-looking version of his brother Arthur.

He stood up and placed a black briefcase on the table in front of him. Then he opened the case to reveal four jewels on a field of black velvet: the Martha Washington ruby, the diamond, the emerald, and the Atkinson sapphire.

The room got quiet as everyone stared at the jewels, which gleamed beautifully against the black background.

"How did you get them?" Erin asked.

"As you know, there is not enough evidence to prosecute my brother," Mr. Atkinson answered. "But our family has removed him from his position at the school. And we convinced him to turn over the four jewels, in exchange for not cutting him out of the family completely. Fortunately, he hadn't sold them yet. He was waiting to make sure you kids were right about the treasure."

"So what will happen to them now?" Jasmine asked.

"The sapphire will remain at Atkinson, of course," he said. "And the emerald will be returned to its owner, Derrica Girard. Our family has decided to donate the diamond to the Metropolitan Museum of Art, where it was found. And the ruby is now back where it belongs."

He reached in the case, picked up the ruby necklace, and handed it to Principal Frederickson. The principal smiled, and gazed happily around at the assembled crowd. Just then she noticed the yearning look in Jasmine's eyes.

"Would you like to hold it before I put it back?" she asked.

"Yes, please," Jasmine said breathlessly.

Principal Frederickson gently placed it in Jasmine's open palm as her friends gathered around her. Jasmine had always admired the stone, sketching it countless times. She had only ever seen it underneath glass.

"It's so beautiful," she whispered.

"It is good to have it back here at the school," Principal Frederickson said. "But even so, I wish you girls had not put yourselves in danger like that. And I am sure your parents feel the same way."

The four Jewels exchanged glances. All of their parents had been called to the school once they got back from Mount Vernon, and they had tried to explain the events as best as they could. As a result, they were in varying degrees of trouble. Erin and Willow were both grounded from after-school activities for a week, and Lili's parents had nearly banned her from participating on the quiz bowl team. Jasmine's parents were curious, asking question after question. It almost seemed like Jasmine's mom wished she could have joined in the fun.

"Don't worry," Willow said. "Our days of tracking jewel thieves and chasing treasure are over. We've got more important things to worry about." She looked at her friends.

"Nationals!" they all cheered at once.

Chapter Nineteen

"We really should be studying for Nationals," Willow said a little worriedly as the Jewels walked the grounds of Mount Vernon a few days later.

"Willow, we've been studying nonstop for a week," Erin reminded her. "We need a break."

"Besides, we never got a really good look at the treasure," Jasmine added. "I am dying of curiosity!"

"It's amazing that Mount Vernon put it on display so fast," Lili remarked.

Willow nodded. "Everyone's been so curious about it, they decided to put it out to meet the demand," she said. "Then I read that they're going to send it on tour to museums around the country."

Jasmine shivered. "I still can't believe that we helped find it. It seems like a dream, doesn't it?"

Erin nodded. "It does. And what's even more unbelievable is that we're friends with the Rivals."

"No kidding," Lili agreed. "Did I hear you and Isabel making plans for a sleepover the other day?"

Erin gave a sheepish grin. "There's a twenty-four-hour Civil War marathon on the History Channel coming up," she said. "It's no fun watching those alone."

"It's no fun watching those *ever*," Lili teased.

Jasmine's mother, who had driven them to the museum, followed behind on the grass-lined path. She nodded toward a small brick building up ahead. "There's the museum, girls."

A line of people snaked outside the entrance to the Donald W. Reynolds Museum.

"Wow, the black opal is really popular," Jasmine remarked.

"Of course it is," Erin said. "It's an awesome discovery."

The line to see the treasure was a separate line from the museum entrance. Inside the museum, visitors could see personal items that belonged to the Washingtons, as well as paintings and sculptures. But today, everyone had come to see the black opal.

After a fifteen-minute wait, the girls and Mrs. Johnson finally reached the glass display case, where the black opal sat inside.

"It's even more amazing up close," Jasmine said, getting as near to the glass as she could. "I wish I had gotten a better look when I held it in my hand."

"It's like the more you look, the more colors you see," Lili said breathlessly. "I don't think I've ever seen anything so beautiful!"

"I still think it's so cool that Martha came up with all those clues and had them etched on the jewels," Jasmine remarked. "That was really smart."

"That's what I've been trying to tell you guys. She was a pretty awesome lady," Erin said.

"We should move on, girls," Jasmine's mom said. "There are a lot of people waiting behind us."

With a sigh, Jasmine broke away from the display, and all of the girls reluctantly left the opal behind. They headed to the food court, a lovely glass pavilion surrounded by a brick terrace with metal tables and chairs. They found an empty table and sat down next to a freshly green bush, where a yellow butterfly rested on top of the leaves.

"I saw online that they have a nice deli here," said Mrs. Johnson. "Who wants a sandwich?"

"Tuna, please," said Lili.

"Oh, make mine tuna, too," Willow said. "Fish is brain food, and my brain needs all the food it can get for tomorrow."

"I'll take a veggie sandwich, if they have one, Mom," Jasmine said.

Mrs. Johnson nodded. "What about you, Erin?"

"Ham, salami, cheese, turkey, tomato, lettuce, pickles, mayo, and mustard, please," Erin said. "On whole wheat."

Lili made a face. "That doesn't sound like brain food."

"Hey, I'm getting it on whole wheat," Erin protested. "That's healthy."

Willow sighed. "It probably doesn't matter what we eat. There are fifteen other teams competing in our category at Nationals, and one of them is the Rivals. We don't have a chance of winning the whole thing."

Jasmine frowned. "That doesn't sound like the Willow I know. You're our math expert. There's got to be some percentage of a chance, right?"

"Well, I haven't fully worked it out yet . . . but yes," Willow grudgingly admitted. "I just feel like we need to study more."

"Then we'll go to the library for another study session as soon as we get back," Jasmine said. She looked at Erin and Lili. "Right?"

Now it was Erin's turn to sigh, but she and Lili still gave the same answer.

"Right!" they said.

Willow smiled. "You know, no matter how we do tomorrow, we should be proud," she said. "We've had a great season."

"And we found Martha's treasure," Erin added. "I'd say it doesn't get much better than that."

"But we *will* win, and things will get even more awesome," Lili said confidently. She held out her right arm over the table.

"Arts and literature!" she cheered.

Erin put her right hand on top of Lili's. "History!"

"Science!" Jasmine said, adding her hand to the pile.

Willow put her hand on top of Jasmine's. "Math!"

Then the four girls cheered together.

"Goooooooooo Jewels!"

Chapter Twenty

"Eight to the third power is five hundred and twelve," Willow said.

"That is correct, and the Jewels are twenty points in the lead so there is no need for a follow-up question," announced the moderator. "The Jewels will be moving on to the next round."

Willow, Jasmine, Erin, and Lili walked across the stage and shook hands with the members of the opposing team. Then they ran off-stage and erupted into squeals.

"We did it!" Willow cheered. "We're going into the finals!"

"I can't believe it," Jasmine said. "My hands are shaking."

Sixteen sixth-grade teams had started competing that morning. First, each team competed against one another. Then the winners of those eight matches competed in the second round. In the third round, the top four teams paired up to compete. Now there were only two teams left: the Jewels and the Rivals.

The kids from the New Jersey team they had just defeated approached them.

"Good match," said Zinnira, the team captain.

"Yeah, you guys know your stuff," said another member, Grace.

The girl next to her nodded. "I'm kind of relieved that you won," Nadia said. "Those Rivals are scary."

The last member of the team, Josemanuel, nodded. "Yeah, they're like robots."

"We used to feel that way, too," Erin said. "But they're pretty normal once you get to know them."

"We even beat them once," Jasmine said.

Zinnira looked impressed. "Nice. Well, good luck!"

"Thanks," Willow replied.

There was a short break before the final round, so the Jewels headed to the lounge backstage at the Kennedy Center Opera House, where the Nationals tournament was taking place. Ms. Keatley was waiting for them with a big smile on her face.

"I am so proud of you!" she said, hugging each of them. "You are tearing through this competition."

On the other side of the room, Mr. Haverford was in a huddle with the four Rivals. Ryan looked up when he saw the Jewels enter.

"Great job," he said. "I'm glad it's you guys we're going up against."

"Why? Because you think we're easy to beat?" Willow asked, suddenly feeling defensive.

"No way," Ryan said. "Because you're worthy competitors."

Willow's angry expression softened. "Thanks. You, too."

Aaron walked up to them. "You guys look nice," he said.

"Thanks," Willow said. "Lili came up with our outfits, like always."

Because Nationals was being held in the classic and rather fancy Kennedy Center Opera House, Lili had decided that their usual T-shirts just wouldn't cut it. Instead, they each wore a ruby-red blouse with a black skirt and shoes. .

"They are much better than those glittery shirts you wear," Isabel remarked.

"We've still got glitter," Erin said, pointing to the sparkling pin on her collar. "Lili made one for each of us in honor of the four jewels. Mine's blue, like the sapphire, see? Jasmine's looks like rubies, Willow's is diamonds, and Lili's got a green emerald."

Veronica stepped up and got a closer look at Erin's pin. Lili had created a swirly design using blue glass jewels.

"Wow, that's cool," she said admiringly.

"I can make some for you, too!" Lili said. "After all, we found the jewels together."

"That would be nice," Veronica agreed.

Lili turned to the boys. "Don't worry. I'll make you some cufflinks or something."

A young woman wearing a headset walked into the lounge. "You guys are back onstage in five minutes," she said.

Jasmine's palms immediately began to sweat. "Oh my gosh! I can't believe we're in the finals!"

Ryan held out his hand to Willow. "May the best team win!"

The Jewels and Rivals solemnly shook hands with one another, and then headed back onstage.

Ever after a full day of competing there, the opera house still felt like the most magnificent stage they'd ever been on. The hall was huge, with three levels of balconies. The seats and balcony facades were a rich red velvet.

"It's like being inside a ruby," Jasmine whispered as they walked back to their microphones.

"I just realized that, too," Erin whispered back. "Maybe that's good luck!"

The quiz bowl moderator was already standing at the lectern. There was a different moderator for this round, and this time a woman with short gray hair and glasses had the job.

"Welcome to the last round of the Grade Six National Quiz Bowl

Championship," she announced. "Competing today are the Atkinson Preparatory Rivals and the Martha Washington Jewels, both from the Washington, DC, area."

A cheer went up from the crowd. It was hard to see faces because of the bright lights on stage, but Willow shaded her eyes to make sure Principal Frederickson, Ms. Keatley, and all their parents were still there. Seeing her mom's face always made her feel a little bit calmer.

"The rules are the same as the previous rounds," the moderator went on. "The first team to buzz in after a question has the opportunity to answer. If the answer is correct, they will be asked three follow-up questions. If the answer is incorrect, the other team will have a chance to respond."

Willow tightened her hand around her buzzer, and looked down the row at her teammates. Jasmine, Erin, and Lili were all doing the same. They were ready to go.

"First question," the moderator began. "A book is on sale for fifteen dollars. If the sale price is twenty-five percent off the original cost, what was the original price?"

Another math question, Willow thought, and she quickly did the calculations in her head. She buzzed in — one second later than Ryan.

"Twenty dollars," Ryan replied.

"Correct," the moderator said, and Willow felt her stomach flip. Was this how the rest of the match was going to go?

The Rivals got three follow-up math questions right, and with each question worth ten points, they were leading the Jewels 40–0 right out of the gate. Willow gripped the buzzer even more tightly.

"What is the scientific name that describes rocks that have melted and then cooled and solidified?" the moderator asked.

Jasmine hit the buzzer so quickly that Willow nearly jumped out of her skin.

"Igneous!" she practically shouted when the moderator called on her.

"Correct," she said. "And now for your follow-up questions."

The next three questions were also about geology, Jasmine's specialty, and the score was now tied at 40–40.

The next question was about the Little House on the Prairie books, and Aaron got to it before Lili could buzz in. Willow was starting to feel a sense of déjà vu. Every time they faced the Rivals, it was like a tennis match. The Rivals got one right, and then the Jewels got one right. If the Rivals missed a follow-up question, the Jewels missed one on their next turn.

It's going to be right down to the last question, Willow thought. She could feel it. With the Rivals, there was always going to be suspense.

And Willow was right.

"This is the last toss-up question," the moderator said as the match drew to a close. "The Jewels and Rivals are tied, so if one team gives the correct answer to this question they will win the match — and the Grade Six National Quiz Bowl Championship."

A hush went over the crowd as the moderator picked up the last card — the card that would decide everything.

"Name the lawyer who wrote the lyrics to the United States' national anthem, 'The Star-Spangled Banner,'" the moderator said.

Erin and Isabel buzzed in at what sounded like almost exactly the same time. The moderator looked to one of the judges offstage, who walked on and conferred with her. Willow's heart was beating like a drum.

"Martha Washington gets the question," the moderator said, and Willow let out a huge sigh of relief.

Erin grinned. "That would be Francis Scott Key."

"Correct," the moderator said. "Congratulations, Jewels. You are the Grade Six National Quiz Bowl Champions!"

This time, the girls couldn't hold back their cheering. They jumped up and down, hugging one another. A man in a suit walked onstage with a three-foot-tall trophy that he placed in Willow's arms.

The Rivals walked over to them.

"I can't say I'm happy we lost," Veronica said. "But at least you guys won."

"Thanks!" Willow said. "It was hard beating you guys."

"Yeah, it came right down to the wire there," Erin said, looking at Isabel.

"It was *too* close," Isabel said with a grin. "We will beat you next time."

Both teams posed for photos for their excited parents before heading backstage to gather their things and leave. Willow placed the trophy on a table and everyone gathered around to admire it.

"It's so shiny," Lili said, touching the silver cup.

"I like the design of the plaque," Jasmine said, pointing to a black plate engraved with symbols for science, math, history, and the arts. Then Jasmine frowned. "Wait, there's something sticking out from behind the plaque."

Jasmine tugged at a piece of yellow paper tucked behind the engraved plate and pulled out a small, folded note. She opened it up to reveal a message that looked like it had been typed on an old typewriter.

> *The four lost jewels have all been found,*
> *But many treasures still abound.*

Willow looked at Ryan. "Very cute. When did you plant this?"

Ryan shook his head. "I didn't." And Willow started smiling in disbelief.

"I swear, I didn't!" he insisted

"Of course you did," Jasmine said. "It's on the same lined paper as those notes you sent us before."

"But the writing is different," Erin pointed out, and silence descended on the group.

Lili's eyes were wide. "Well, if Ryan didn't send it, then who did?" she asked.

The Jewels and Rivals looked at one another questioningly, but no one had an answer.

"Don't tell me we have more jewels to find," Jasmine said, but her voice sounded more hopeful than complaining.

Erin put a finger to her lips. "Shhh, don't let Principal Frederickson hear you say that," she said, and everyone laughed.

"Seriously, guys, what if we get another message?" Lili asked.

"Then we'll do what we do best, and try to figure it out," Willow said. "After all, we're the Jewels!"

"*And* the Rivals!" Ryan chimed in. All eight teammates looked at one another and grinned. They would do it together!

The End

SNIFF OUT MYSTERIES, DIG UP CLUES,

Collar the CULPRIT...

a DOG and his GIRL MYSTERIES

Play DEAD

Jane B. Mason and Sarah Hines Stephens

SCHOLASTIC

...DON'T MISS

a DOG and his GIRL
MYSTERIES